DUKE LOOKS LIKE A GROOMSMAN

THE FOOTMEN'S CLUB SERIES

VALERIE BOWMAN

JUNE THIRD ENTERPRISES, LLC

Duke Looks Like a Groomsman, copyright ® 2020 by June Third Enterprises, LLC.

Print edition ISBN: 978-0-9893758-7-0

Digital edition ISBN: 978-0-9893758-4-9

Book Cover Design © Lyndsey Llewellen at Llewellen Designs.

For my friend Vickie Lambert, who I miss every day.

Colon Cancer Coalition: Colon Cancer Nonprofit
coloncancercoalition.org

He's posing as a groomsman

Rhys Sheffield, the Duke of Worthington, has bet his friends an ungodly sum of money that despite his loftiness, he can pass himself off as a servant at *the* house party of the Season. But when his clever ex-flame arrives and recognizes Rhys in the stables pretending to be a groomsman, she realizes it's the perfect opportunity to pay him back for breaking off their engagement.

She's the bride-to-be

The lovely Lady Julianna Montgomery may be the only young woman at the house party who's *not* in the market for a husband. She's quite happily engaged to a marquess, thank you very much, and scarcely remembers the pain of being callously tossed over by the Duke of Worthington nearly two long years ago—till now.

All bets are off

Rhys seems to be everywhere, flexing his muscles, laboring in the sun—and Julianna has never found him more appealing. With his signature charm, he persuades her to keep his secret. But when she learns he's determined to win a bet of honor, she can't resist playing a game of her own. She'll spend the next fortnight tempting Rhys at every turn *and* making him lose his precious wager. Even if it means she must lose her heart in the process...

THE PLAYERS

Lucas Drake, the Earl of Kendall
Dark-brown-haired, green-eyed, former navy hero turned earl, who needs to find a lady to make a countess. His friends cook up an insane plot to help him.

Rhys Sheffield, the Duke of Worthington
(aka Worth)
Black-haired, dark-blue-eyed, devil-may-care rake and gambler with a love of horses. He's tall, dark, and handsome and has a past with a certain lady, who may just be bent on revenge when the perfect opportunity presents itself.

Beaumont Bellham, the Marquess of Bellingham
(aka Bell)
Blond-haired, light-blue-eyed, in control of everything in his world. Bell is a spy for the Home Office, and nothing misses his notice, that is until he just might meet his match in the most unexpected of places.

Miss Frances Wharton, daughter of Baron Winfield
Brown-haired and eyed, she's determined to fight for the rights of the poor, has a tiny dowry, reads too much, and is too particular according to her mother. Frances has no interest in marriage until she meets a footman who just might change her mind.

Lady Julianna Montgomery, daughter of the Duke of Montlake
Blond-haired, light-green-eyed Lady Julianna is gorgeous,

rich, and comes from an excellent family. Once considered the best catch of the Season, she's happily engaged to the Marquess of Murdock. But when she finds her ex-flame, Worth, pretending to be a groom in the stables at a house party, she decides it's the perfect opportunity to pay him back for jilting her.

Ewan Fairchild, Viscount Clayton
Boon companion to Kendall, Worth, and Bell, and host of the infamous summer house party. Married to his true love, Theodora, whom he met when she broke her leg trying to sneak into his stables.

AUTHOR'S NOTE

The Footmen's Club Series includes the stories of the Earl of Kendall (book 1, *The Footman and I*), the Duke of Worthington (book 2, *Duke Looks Like a Groomsman*), and the Marquess of Bellingham (book 3, *The Valet Who Loved Me*).

The prologue of the first three books is the same scene written from each hero's point of view. Rest assured, with the exception of the prologue, no other content or scene is repeated.

If you *haven't* read the other books, the prologue will help you understand the origin of The Footmen's Club. If you *have* read the other books, the prologue will give you a bit more insight into the hero of that book.

Thanks for reading!

Valerie

PROLOGUE

London, July 1814

Rhys Sheffield, the Duke of Worthington, was having a fine evening. True, that all his evenings were fine, as they usually included drinks with friends and then a jaunt to Hollister's gaming hell where he often lost a small fortune in the span of a few hours. Tonight, he was enjoying the drinks-with-friends portion of the evening at the Curious Goat Inn. A decent little place outside of Mayfair where he and Kendall, Bell, and Clayton could drink and talk freely without being scrutinized by the other members of the *ton*. The Curious Goat was much preferred to any of those stodgy gentlemen's clubs on St. James's Street.

Just before they'd entered the establishment, his friends had all exclaimed how glad they were to have him back to his old self. Until somewhat recently, he'd been someone different entirely. The headaches were a regular reminder. But that was something he didn't relish thinking about, something he pushed to the back of his mind every chance he got.

Rhys was ordering his third ale of the evening from a comely barmaid when Kendall, of all unexpected people, blurted, "I think it's time I find a wife."

The heads of all three of them, himself, Bell, and Clayton, immediately snapped to face Kendall. They stared at the chap as if he'd lost his bloody mind.

Never at a loss for words, Rhys found his voice first. He winced, sucked in his breath, shook his head vigorously, and said, "A *wife*? Good God, man! There's no need to rush into anything so...*permanent*."

Kendall was a good man. After they'd all left Oxford together, Kendall had gone on to become a Commodore in His Majesty's Royal Navy. But he hadn't been gifted a commission by his father, the former earl. No. Kendall had worked his arse off. There was no one more diligent or more loyal. But the poor sop actually wanted a *wife*. Kendall should know better after his last attempt at marriage with the disloyal Lady Emily Foswell. Had he forgotten about her defection?

"We're not getting any younger," Kendall shot back to Rhys.

"On the contrary," Rhys replied, "at nine and twenty, we're pups. My father was over *fifty* when I was born."

His father had famously remained a bachelor for decades before settling down with his (much younger) mother, and dutifully producing Rhys. Of course, having begotten his heir, his father decided to continue his bachelor lifestyle, leaving Rhys's resigned mother to her own amusements, of which she'd found plenty. As a result, Rhys had mainly been raised by servants, governesses, and tutors.

His father would return to the ducal estate upon occasion to see how Rhys was growing, to ensure his son understood the enormity of his title, and to give him advice about women that Rhys seriously doubted was sound.

It certainly hadn't helped the one time that Rhys had come close to offering for a lady. A fate he'd narrowly escaped, having discovered the lady in question was interested in him only for his title. *That* was something else he pushed to the back of his mind every chance he got.

Bell, or more correctly, Beaumont Bellham, the Marquess of Bellingham, was the next to speak to Kendall. Bell might have been a bachelor, but the man was essentially married to his position as a spy in the Home Office. The fool had even tried to renounce his title for a spot as a soldier in the wars against France. Thank God, he'd been turned down in his request.

Instead, he'd been offered a position with the Home Office, where he was kept safe enough most of the time. Though Bell had been on some dangerous missions before and Rhys knew it.

Bell was clever, direct, and driven. If the man had any fault, it was that he worked too much, for Christ's sake. The marquess needed to relax more than anyone Rhys had ever known, and Rhys told him that often enough. Instead of taking such sound advice, however, Bell attempted to tell Rhys that *he* might try an honest day's work instead of spending his time gaming and chasing women. Who needed *that* sort of advice?

Bell narrowed his eyes on Kendall and said, "Are you certain you're ready? It's only been two years since…." Bell let his voice trail off, but they all knew he was talking about Lady Emily. The look on Kendall's face told him to leave it alone.

Finally, Clayton exclaimed, "Thank heavens. I cannot wait until I'm no longer the only one of us with the parson's noose around his neck."

Rhys laughed at that. Clayton had recently got himself leg-shackled. On purpose. The viscount loved science and creating things. He was extremely wealthy, had yet to meet a stranger, and was an active member of Parliament. He was the last one they'd all thought would be first to marry. But even Rhys had to admit that marriage seemed to agree with the chap. Clayton had just returned from his honeymoon and he still appeared to be deeply in love with his wife, Theodora. Who knew? Perhaps love was a thing after all. At least for some gentlemen.

Rhys took a draught from his mug and glanced around at his three friends. The four of them had met at Eton as lads and stuck together come what may. Each of them played a unique role in their group.

These days Kendall was distracted by the bill he was trying to get passed in Parliament. The Employment Bill was a piece of legislation that his older brother had sponsored before dying of consumption and leaving the earldom to Kendall.

Bell was obsessed with chasing after a traitor who had betrayed the English army at Bidassoa in Spain, and Clayton was busy as usual, hosting parties and playing politics, the two things he did best.

Rhys was well aware that he was the devil-may-care ne'er-do-well of the lot. He kept up his steady stream of drinking, gambling, and chasing women. That was what the *ton* expected of the Duke of Worthington, after all, and that's what they got from him. He was one in a long line of dukes who spent more time seeing to their own pleasures than the details of their estates. That was what solicitors were for, after all, and Rhys had a fine solicitor. He even met with the man nearly daily to hear the boring details as to how his properties were running. What more could he be asked to do? Life was for living, after all, not keeping one's head inside a tedious book of figures. Or any book for that matter. No matter how much Bell teased him for not reading, Rhys remained convinced just about *anything* was more fun.

Rhys had a head for figures, but instead of using it to run his estates, he used it at the gambling table. Only far too often he was too deep in his cups at the gambling table and he lost. But no matter. What was lost today might easily be won again tomorrow. That was the beauty of gaming. There was always a second chance. Quite unlike marriage.

If one made a bad marriage, one was stuck for life. And, as he'd learned, some women were nothing more than scheming liars looking to spear the biggest fish. And in their world, the glittering *beau monde*, the biggest fish meant the man with the best title. Outside of royalty, there was no better title than duke, of course. *That* had been drilled into Rhys's head by his father from the time he was barely able to walk. Rhys had to be especially careful when it came to the fairer sex.

And he had been. Or so he thought.

Unlike Kendall, at least Rhys hadn't actually *offered* for the woman he'd nearly fallen for. Rhys had always been suspicious of Lady Emily Foswell for Kendall's sake, however. The woman had never seemed particularly pleased to see Kendall. And when she tossed him over on the eve of their wedding for a baron, Rhys had been incensed. Angrier, even, than Kendall himself.

Kendall, who, at the time, had been a second son in the Navy, had taken the news with a sort of resigned unhappiness, but Rhys, Rhys had been prepared to go find the woman and give her a speech on the importance of loyalty and the treachery of greed. Not that *he* should be lecturing anyone on anything, but Kendall had every right.

The one thing that consoled Rhys was the fact that now Lady Emily had to live the rest of her life knowing she'd inadvertently tossed over a future earl for a baron. Ha.

"I'm entirely serious," Kendall continued. "I must look to secure the earldom. I fear I've been too preoccupied with the Employment Bill. I've been remiss waiting this long to find a bride."

"I certainly won't disagree with you that you've been too preoccupied with the Employment Bill," Rhys replied with a snort. "'Obsessed' is more like it."

Kendall shrugged. "Well, now that the Lords have tabled the vote until the autumn session, I have more time to rally the support I need. I might as well get about the business of looking for a wife in earnest."

"I never bother to vote in Parliament," Rhys replied. "Don't happen to care for the hours. And all the arguing is downright exhausting."

Bell gave him a beleaguered look and shook his head. "God forbid you take an interest in your seat or any of the issues the country is dealing with."

Rhys gave them his most charming grin. "I'm entirely confident you chaps can handle it," he replied, clapping Bell on the back.

"When the time comes for the vote for my brother's bill," Kendall continued, addressing his remarks to Rhys, "I'll drive to your town house and drag you out of bed myself."

Bell's and Clayton's laughter filled the alcove in which they were sitting. His friends knew Rhys disliked anything that involved his waking early in the morning.

I'd like to see you try. But Rhys decided to keep that particular thought to himself.

"Let's not talk of such unpleasantness," Rhys replied with a sigh. "You mentioned finding a bride, Kendall. That's much more interesting. Now, how old are you again?" He shoved back in his chair and crossed his arms over his chest, narrowing his eyes at the earl.

Rhys knew as well as the rest of them that they were the

same age save for a matter of months. He loved to pretend he'd forgotten how old they were. *Age is a number without meaning.* A line his father had often used.

Kendall arched his brow. "The same age you are, old man."

"Well, then," Rhys declared. "You've plenty of time to find a wife as far as I'm concerned."

"That's easy to say, coming from a man who's never given a toss about securing his *own* title," Kendall shot back, with a good-natured grin.

Rhys returned the smile with a devilish one of his own. "I cannot argue with you there." He turned and gave the barmaid his even more charming smile, the one he saved exclusively for women, as he ordered another round of ale for the table.

"Yes, well, if you're seriously looking for a wife, Kendall, the Season has just ended," Clayton interjected. "It seems you've missed your chance. The entire *ton* is about to retire to the country as soon as Parliament closes next week."

"I'm well aware," Kendall replied with a curt nod. "The Season makes my skin crawl. Full of simpering maids and purse-eyeing mamas eager to show off their best behavior in the hopes of snaring a rich husband. I don't want to find a wife that way."

"How else do you intend to find one?" Bell's eyes were narrowed. The marquess was up to something, Rhys could tell.

"I don't know how exactly." Kendall took another drink. "But this time I intend to find a lady who loves me for myself."

There it was. Kendall's only allowance to the Lady Emily debacle. Well, at least he'd learned his lesson. Rhys, of course, had no idea how one would go about finding a woman who 'loves me for myself.' It sounded quite impossible to him, but at least it was the correct attitude. Thank Christ his friend was finally seeing reason.

"Yes!" Rhys pounded his fist against the table, his voice filling with anger. "I think we can all agree that Lady Emily is the lowest of the low. There's no excuse for what she did, tossing over one man for another with a better title. As far as I'm concerned, she no longer exists."

"Can we *not* discuss Lady Emily, please?" Kendall groaned and covered his face with one hand.

The barmaid reappeared with the drinks and Rhys's smile reappeared too. "Keep 'em coming, Love," he said to her, before turning back to Kendall and adding, "I'm merely pointing out that if you want a lady who loves you for yourself, the Season and its ridiculousness are the last place you should go."

"Yes," Kendall replied with a sigh, lifting his mug into the air to salute Rhys. "Didn't I already say that? The Season and its *fetes are* the last place I should go, which is why I've avoided it like the pox for the last two Seasons."

"Oh, is *that* why you haven't attended the boring balls at Almack's?" Rhys replied with a smirk. "I thought it was the tepid tea and small talk. That's why I steer clear of them."

"You avoid them because they don't serve brandy and we all know it," Bell pointed out, staring fixedly at Rhys, his arms crossed tightly over his chest.

Rhys winked at his friend. He wasn't about to deny it. "That and they won't give me the bank that Hollister's will."

Kendall scratched his chin and stared blindly at his mug. "If only the ladies of the *ton* didn't know I am an earl, I'd have a much better chance of finding a match," he grumbled.

Rhys's laughter cracked off the wooden beams on the tavern's ceiling. "I'd pay to see *that*. An earl dressed up like a common man to find *true love*. Has a certain poetic ring to it, don't it?"

Clayton laughed too and shook his head, while Bell's shrewd, narrowed-eyed stare intensified. "It's not a *completely* outlandish idea." He tilted his head to the side.

"What's not?" Kendall asked.

"The idea of pretending you're a commoner to find a wife," Bell replied.

Rhys slapped Bell on the back. "Are you mad, man? You're not even *drinking*."

Of course Bell wasn't drinking. The man never drank. Most annoying thing about him. The marquess preferred to remain in control of his faculties, and they all knew it. He'd always been the one to remain out of any fracas the other three got into, usually due to his sobriety.

Bell leaned forward and stared at Kendall. "Given the right circumstances, it could work, you know?"

"Pretending I'm common?" Kendall replied, blinking. "I don't see how."

"Everyone in the *ton* knows him," Clayton pointed out. "How would he ever manage it?"

Hmm. Was Bell actually serious? Rhys stared intently at his friend. He was serious, wasn't he? Why, this could be interesting. *Quite* interesting, indeed.

"Are you suggesting he wear a mask or alter his appearance?" Rhys asked, narrowing his eyes just like Bell. Could this actually work?

Kendall glanced back and forth between Rhys and Bell. "You cannot be serious, either of you. Clayton's right. How would it ever work?"

"No, not a costume." Bell addressed his remarks to Rhys. "I was thinking something more like the right...situation."

"Such as?" Rhys replied, drawing out both words. He also leaned forward.

"You two are frightening me, you know?" Kendall replied.

"You seem as if you're actually trying to plot out a way this ludicrous idea might work."

"Like a...house party," Bell replied to Rhys, stroking his own chin and completely ignoring Kendall's concern.

Rhys inclined his head, his eyes still narrowed. "A house party, yes. I see what you mean."

"But it couldn't be just *any* house party, of course," Bell continued. "It would have to be one given by someone who was in on the experiment."

"'Experiment'?" Clayton perked up. "There are few things I enjoy more than an experiment, and I just so happen to be about to send the invitations to my annual country house party."

"'Experiment'?" Kendall repeated, blinking.

Bell snapped his fingers. "Your house party would be perfect, Clayton."

"Wait. Wait. Wait. Wait. Wait." Kendall, who sat between Bell and Rhys, pushed against their shoulders with both hands. He was clearly becoming concerned that they were serious. And they were *quite* serious. "A house party isn't going to change my identity. Ladies of the *ton* will still know who I am at a house party."

"He makes a good point," Clayton replied, sloshing more ale down his throat. Leave it to Clayton to try to be reasonable. The man simply didn't have the imagination Bell and Rhys did. Poor chap.

"Not if you invite only the debutantes from this Season," Bell replied, a smug smile tugging at his lips. "And not if you create the right circumstances."

Kendall sucked in a deep breath and pushed his mug out of reach. "The ladies may not know me, but some of their mothers do. More than one of them has already been to court with an older daughter making her debut."

"That's where the right *circumstances* come in," Bell

replied, crossing his arms over his chest, the half-smile still riding his lips.

Rhys scratched at the day-old stubble on his chin and smiled an even wider smile than Bell's. "By God, I think you're onto something."

"I refuse to wear a mask if that's what you're thinking. That's positively medieval," Kendall declared, shaking his head.

"Not a mask," Bell replied. He settled back in his chair and plucked at his lower lip, a gesture he often made when he was plotting something.

"Or a costume, either," Kendall continued. He pushed his mug farther away. Probably for good measure. No doubt the poor chap was trying to sober up. Ha.

"Not a costume...precisely." Bell exchanged a positively roguish grin with Rhys.

"By God, I'm going to have the *best* time watching this," Rhys said, nodding.

"Watching what?" Clayton's nose was scrunched in confusion. "I don't know what in the devil either of you is talking about any longer."

"I'm talking about Kendall here pretending to be a servant," Bell replied, still grinning.

Kendall blinked. "A servant?"

"Yes. It's perfect," Rhys added, nodding.

Kendall turned to him and stared as if he'd lost his mind. "Perfect? Me? Being a servant? How is that perfect?"

"That still doesn't fix the problem of the ladies' mothers recognizing him. Even if he's dressed as a servant," Clayton pointed out.

"Ah, but it does," Bell replied. "That's the beauty of it. Most people don't look at servants. They don't pay attention to the majority of things beyond what they need and want. My training as a spy has taught me much about the human failure to notice details. I'd be willing to bet that not one of those ladies of the *ton* will look twice at Kendall if he's dressed as a servant and performing servants' duties. He'll be wearing livery, knee breeches, and a powdered wig, after all."

"And it has the added advantage that a servant will be in a particularly excellent position to discover how a lady truly behaves," Rhys added, sweeping his long dark hair off his forehead with his fingers. "I'd wager she's at her best when addressing a potential bridegroom and at her worst when addressing a servant. God knows I've seen it time and again from my mother."

"You're both truly mad, you know that?" Kendall replied, looking positively alarmed.

"I dunno," Clayton replied, tugging at his cravat. "But it sounds like quite a lark to me. I'm perfectly willing to offer my upcoming house party as a venue for such an experiment."

"You've gone mad too, then," Kendall declared.

"Think about it," Bell said, turning his attention to Kendall. "It has the potential to give you precisely what you want. An unencumbered look at the latest crop of debutantes behaving precisely how they would when they don't know you are watching."

Kendall narrowed his eyes on the marquess. "It's positively alarming that you don't see the problem with this plan."

Bell shrugged. "What problem? The risk is not too great. If anyone recognizes you, we'll simply ask that person to play along. No doubt they'll enjoy the game too."

"What if I find a lady I fancy?" Kendall replied. "Am I supposed to simply rip off my livery and declare myself an earl and expect she'll fall madly in love with me?"

"Not at all," Bell said. "I'm merely suggesting that you get to *know* these young ladies on the basis of how they treat servants. I've no doubt the best-natured ones will be kind and pleasant. Once you have a few candidates, you will know who to court next Season."

Kendall shook his head slowly. He pulled his mug back toward his chest at last. Perhaps he was beginning to like the idea. "You're suggesting that I choose a future bride on the basis of how she treats a footman?"

Bell arched a brow. "How did Lady Emily treat servants?" His next words were slow and deliberate.

Kendall clenched his jaw.

Rhys pursed his lips. Now *that* had been a good point. Bell always knew precisely what to say. Lady Emily had snapped at a servant a time or two. They'd all witnessed it.

"I see by the look on your face that you recognize my point," Bell drawled.

Kendall appeared to consider it for a moment. Rhys could tell by the dawning look on his face that he was beginning to see the merits in the plan. He had to be. The man needed a wife. How better to find one you could trust?

"I'm willing to do it with you," Bell tossed out casually with another shrug.

"What?" Rhys snapped his eyebrows together. "Why would *you* do it?"

Bell straightened his shoulders and settled back into his chair. "Because I've narrowed down my hunt for the Bidassoa traitor to one of three possibilities."

"The man you've been hunting for the Home Office?" Rhys clarified, lowering his voice.

"Precisely the one," Bell replied. "And if Clayton here will invite those three men to the house party, I will also pretend to be a servant to watch them."

Rhys tossed back his head and laughed. "I should have known you had another motive all along, Bell. His Majesty's work is never far from your mind. Even when we're drinking."

Bell's grin widened. "Why shouldn't we use the opportunity for two useful pursuits instead of one? I'll admit, I was already thinking about this plan before Kendall informed us of his search for a wife, but if it helps both of us, all the better, I say. We will truly have to behave as servants, however. We'll have to wait on the guests and do all the tasks servants must do."

"Hmm. I do quite like the idea of spying going on under my roof." Clayton took another long draught of ale. "Gives the whole affair a bit of intrigue. And since I haven't been a soldier or served His Majesty otherwise, I feel it's my duty to say yes to this ruse. Not to mention my love of an experiment. Will you do it, Kendall?"

Kendall hefted his mug to his lips and drained it. Then he wiped the back of his hand across his mouth. "Now that Bell's doing it with me, how can I refuse?"

Rhys accepted yet another new mug of ale from the barmaid and flipped a coin into the air for her tip. He gave her a flirtatious grin before turning his attention back to the conversation. "I, for one, am so interested in seeing such a situation play out, not only will I attend to watch the spectacle, I will also settle a large sum on the outcome as to whether you two can pull this off. Care to bet me?" He gave them both his most competitive stare.

Bell rolled his eyes. "Everything's a bet with you, Worth."

"Perhaps, but you must admit, this is a particularly tempting bet." Rhys lifted his chin toward the marquess. "Five hundred pounds say you are both outed by a keen-eyed mama within a sennight."

"I'll take that bet!" Clayton declared, pointing a finger in the air. "You'll be attending as a guest, I presume, Worthington."

Kendall's snort of laughter interrupted Rhys's reply. "Of course, he's attending as a guest. Our mate Worth here could *never* pass for a footman." He shook his head sympathetically toward the duke. "You couldn't last one night serving others, I'm afraid."

Rhys gathered himself up and straightened his shoulders. "I take offense to that. If you two sops can do it, surely I can."

Clayton blew air into his cheeks and shook his head, not quite meeting Rhys's gaze. "Hmm. I'm not exactly certain I agree with that, old chap."

Rhys crossed his arms over his chest and glared at his friend. "You truly don't think I could do it?"

"No," Clayton admitted, looking slightly sheepish. "Not if you actually have to fill the role of a servant and do real chores. No."

Rhys's gaze swung to Bell. "You don't think I can do it either?" Was this truly what his friends thought of him? He knew he had a reputation to live down, but they didn't think him capable of working as a servant for so much as a fortnight?

Bell shook his head. "Not a chance. Apologies, Your Grace, but you're far too used to being waited upon to wait on anyone else."

"But that's how I know how to do it properly," Rhys shot back, entirely disgruntled.

Kendall snorted. "I'm afraid seeing one serve and actually *serving* are two entirely different things."

Rhys's eyes widened. *That hypocrite.* "You're a bloody earl for Christ's sake. Why do you think *you* can serve?"

"I may be an earl but I'm no stranger to hard work. I spent years in the Navy doing chores like picking oakum and deworming hardtack. And those two tasks were pleasant compared to some of my other tasks," Kendall replied.

Rhys slapped a palm on the tabletop. The mugs bounced.

"Fine. One *thousand* pounds says I can make it through the entire fortnight as a servant too. Or at least I can last longer than either of you."

"Now who is being mad?" Clayton asked, waggling his eyebrows at Rhys.

"I'm quite serious." Rhys's jaw was locked. If he was anything, he was competitive, and he was never more competitive than when someone believed he *couldn't* do something. The thought incensed him. He'd win this bet if it was the last thing he did. "*One thousand* pounds, gentlemen. Who will take the bet?"

"I will," all three called in unison.

CHAPTER ONE

Viscount Clayton's Country Estate,
Devon, August 1814

T hank Christ he'd finally escaped the house. Mrs.
Cotswold, Clayton's housekeeper, could be a
frightening woman when she chose to be, and it
appeared that she chose to be a great deal of the time.

The older woman had been tasked with ensuring the
three noblemen were fit to serve in Clayton's household.
She'd begun their training in London and had continued it
here in the countryside. If Rhys had had any idea of the kind
of strict discipline and watchful eye he'd be under while
pretending to be a servant, he might not have been so quick
to join the 'experiment' (as Clayton liked to call it). But he'd
made his bet, and he never backed down from a bet, Mrs.
Cotswold or no. Besides, the kind of money Rhys had riding
on *this* particular bet meant he couldn't back down even if
Medusa herself was employed as Clayton's housekeeper.

They'd even named their little experiment. *The Footmen's
Club*. Kendall had come up with it. It had a nice ring to it,

only they weren't all going to be footmen. While being fitted for their livery back in London, Rhys had announced to his friends that he intended to be a groomsman instead. Kendall had initially balked at the idea, until Bell had informed him that *he* intended to be a valet. Apparently, valeting would put the marquess in closer proximity to the men he needed to watch.

If Bell could be a valet, then Rhys could be a groomsman. Kendall had grudgingly agreed. Besides, it was only sporting of them to allow Rhys to try his hand at service in the one role he might actually be good at. Horses and stables had long been his favorite place at any estate. And Clayton's stables were particularly fine.

Rhys had had enough of Mrs. Cotswold's harping, however, and finally escaped to the stables to work with his direct supervisor, one Mr. Hereford, the stablemaster.

Rhys was wandering around, wearing his new livery, carrying the bag in which he'd stuffed his clothing and a few necessities, when Mr. Hereford found him.

"Mr. Worthy, I presume?" The older man stepped forward and offered a handshake.

"That's the name for the moment," Rhys replied with a chuckle, offering his own hand.

He liked the stablemaster immediately. Middle-aged with sparkling blue eyes and a ready smile, Mr. Hereford looked as if he'd give Rhys far less grief than Mrs. Cotswold. He'd clearly chosen the correct employment.

"I take it Lord Clayton has informed you of my intentions?" Rhys asked next.

Mr. Hereford nodded. "He did, indeed, Yer Grace."

"No. No, there will be none of that," Rhys replied, shaking his head. "I'm to be Mr. Worthy and no one else while I'm here. No *milord*, no *Your Grace*, and no mentions of dukedoms, if you please."

"Of course, of course, Yer Gra—" Mr. Hereford caught himself and smiled. "Mr. Worthy."

"It'll be especially important when any of the guests are in the stables. And some of them may know who I am so if I'm scarce for a bit, you'll know why."

"Understood," Mr. Hereford replied.

"But I want you to treat me like any other groomsman. I will do my chores and help out around here like everyone else. In fact, I insist upon it."

"Yes, my lor—" Another smile from Mr. Hereford.

Rhys hoisted the bag he carried on his back. "I didn't even bring a trunk. Just this bag with a few belongings. If you'll be so kind as to point me to where I'll sleep, I'll unpack."

"Ye're gonna sleep out 'ere, my lo— Mr. Worthy?" the stablemaster asked, looking more than a bit confused.

"Yes, of course," Rhys replied. "Where do the other stable-hands sleep?"

Mr. Hereford pointed to a staircase. "Up there. Any open berth will do, I suppose."

"Thank you, Mr. Hereford. I'll be back momentarily, and you may show me what chores I should expect to be responsible for."

Mr. Hereford shook his head and turned to leave. But before Rhys had a chance to make it to the staircase, he turned back to look at him. "May I ask ye one more question, Yer Grace? Er, Mr. Worthy?"

"Of course," Rhys replied.

"Lord Clayton didn't say and the rest of us, we're dying ta know. Why exactly are ye doing this?"

"Can't you guess, Mr. Hereford?" Rhys responded with a laugh. "We have a bet. A bet for quite a bit of money."

Mr. Hereford shook his head again and laughed. "Ye're right. I should 'ave guessed."

"Now may I ask you a question?" Rhys replied.

"O' course," the stablemaster responded amiably.

"Do many of the guests come out to the stables when you have this house party? Particularly the debutantes?"

"I wouldn't say many," Mr. Hereford replied, tapping a finger on his chin. "But there's usually one or two wot loves horses more than tea and gossip."

Rhys nodded and turned to climb up the steps. He knew a lady like that, but surely, *she* wouldn't be at this house party. At least he bloody well hoped not.

CHAPTER TWO

Julianna Montgomery looked out toward the tables from her second-floor bedchamber at Viscount Clayton's estate. She and her sister Mary had been placed in one room and Mama in the adjoining one. They'd arrived for the house party just this morning and Mama had insisted they 'rest.'

Julianna had always disliked resting. It was so very uninteresting. She'd much rather be out riding. She traced her fingers along the cool glass of the window and stared off across the gardens and meadow beyond the back of Lord Clayton's estate.

Clayton's stables were renowned in the *ton*. Julianna couldn't wait to get out and see them. If the rumor mill was to be believed, two of his mounts were descended from the famous Godolphin Arabians. The only other nobleman she knew who had a descendant of the Godolphins was… Ugh. The odious, awful, lying Duke of Worthington, also known as Detestable.

Julianna shook her head, chiding herself for thinking of him. He wasn't worth her thoughts. She'd decided that at the beginning of the last Season—*ahem*—her *third* Season. The fact that Detestable was the reason for her being unengaged during her third Season still made her nostrils flare. If that despicable, lying, disingenuous... No! That was not helping. Insults still counted as thinking of him, and she *refused* to do so.

What had she been thinking about before Detestable had entered her thoughts? Oh, yes, horses. The Arabians. They were the only reason she'd agreed to accompany Mama and Mary on this particular jaunt to the countryside after all. Well, that and the fact that Mary had asked for Julianna's help looking for a match. Julianna no longer needed to look for herself now that she was well and truly engaged to the most eligible man in the *ton*. Thank you very much.

Fine, perhaps the Marquess of Murdock was the *third* most eligible if one was being precise. In truth, the good-for-nothing Duke of Worthington was the *most* eligible, but he was a rogue and a scoundrel and a—not helping!

The *second* most eligible gentleman was the Marquess of Bellingham, but he didn't count either. For one reason, he was a confirmed bachelor who'd never expressed the slightest interest in marriage. For another, it was rumored he worked for the Home Office and was deeply engaged in his work. But even if those other two things weren't true, the Marquess of Bellingham was the closest friend of Detestable and *that* alone made him completely unacceptable to her. Julianna wanted nothing to do with *that odious man*.

She'd spent her first Season pining after him and her second Season being wooed by him. Everyone who was anyone within the *ton* had been convinced an engagement between them was imminent. It had even been hinted about in the paper. The *Times* for heaven's sake. So when the duke left for the countryside quite suddenly, directly before the end of her second Season, a bit over a year ago, it had been a shock to everyone, including Julianna, when not only had Worthington *not* offered for her, but he'd cut off their acquaintance entirely.

The last time she'd heard from him, in fact, had been in the form of a poorly written letter many months after his departure, that had offered few details as to his change of heart and absolutely no mention of when she might see him again.

She'd spent a good portion of the first half of her third Season searching every crowd and guest list for him. It wasn't until the Season was half over that Mama, bless her, had sat her down and given her *the talk*. The one Julianna had needed all along. The one in which Mama reminded Julianna that she had two choices in life. She could sit around waiting for Worthington to reappear, or she could act like a true Montgomery and get about the business of securing the *next* most eligible match.

"He's not worth your thoughts," Mama had said during the talk, giving Julianna her new chant, one she repeated to herself over and over in the weeks to come. "Let alone you wasting your best months for him."

Julianna may have gone to her bed that night the tossed-over, would-be intended of the Duke of Worthington, but she'd awakened the next morning the determined, future-intended of the Marquess of Murdock. Murdock was handsome, rich, and charming. Who cared if he wasn't *quite* as handsome, rich, and charming as Detestable?

Julianna had gone on to meet her goal splendidly. By the time her third Season was not three-quarters through, she'd secured her match with Murdock and only suffered a bit of chagrin when the papers implied she'd landed the *next best* bachelor, having let Worthington somehow slip through her fingers.

It irked her of course, but Murdock had never mentioned

it, so what did it matter? It had all been quite tidy, really. Much less trouble than she'd expected. The best part was, now that she was officially betrothed, with her wedding planned for next spring, she could relax at this house party and ride horses as much as she liked, in addition to helping Mary secure a match, of course.

After a promising first Season, her younger sister still had yet to receive an offer, a mistake that would be quickly rectified if Julianna had any say in it. However, first things first.

Julianna glanced at her sister lying on the bed across the room. Her sister's blond hair was fanned across the pillow. Her hazel eyes closed. Yes, Mary was dutifully asleep, and Mama was probably reading. It was the perfect opportunity to find those Arabians.

Besides, there would be time to look for an eligible gentleman for Mary later, at dinner this evening, perhaps. Despite being close friends with Lord Clayton, the Duke of Worthington never attended Clayton's late summer house party. Julianna had looked into the matter before agreeing to come, of course. Apparently, Detestable didn't care for parties filled with debutantes and their mamas. All the better for her.

Julianna glanced around the darkened bedchamber. Mary's chest rose and fell with each breath she took while sleeping. A smile curled Julianna's lips. "I think I'll just go down to the stables," she whispered to herself. "And see about getting a mount."

CHAPTER THREE

A grin covered Rhys's face as he stood in the stables rubbing down Alabaster from his earlier ride. First, he would buy a new *phaeton*. Then, perhaps a set of matching grays to pull it. A new wardrobe would be welcome. And he'd been meaning to do a few things to his property in Kent.

Yes. The money Rhys won from the bet would be welcome, indeed. But even better than spending the money would be *winning* the money. That part was always his favorite. He'd be gracious, of course, informing his friends that they'd put up a good show. Then he would take every single farthing from them. Finally, he'd jaunt down to Hollister's for a bit of sport with his winnings. Mustn't disappoint the gossip rags.

Alabaster stamped his hooves and neighed. Rhys petted the horse's head and spoke softly in his ear. When Clayton had informed Rhys that groomsmen didn't actually *ride* the horses unless they needed to, Rhys had reluctantly agreed. Or appeared to at least. But there was little chance that Rhys would be in the presence of one of Clayton's fine Arabians and not take a ride. Besides, what Clayton didn't know was unlikely to hurt him, wasn't it? Rhys already had an understanding with Mr. Hereford to that effect. Mr. Hereford was an excellent stablemaster, indeed.

It also didn't hurt that all the other groomsmen, stable boys, and coachmen already knew Rhys was the Duke of Worthington. He'd told them, of course. The bet hadn't called for him not to. The only people who mustn't realize he wasn't a groomsman were the guests at the party, the young ladies, specifically, and that would prove simple enough to avoid. He'd been here all day and had yet to see even one young lady in the stables, and the young ladies had been arriving all morning.

It was quite safe actually. The house was full of a lot of simpering debutantes. There was little chance a pampered, chaperoned young woman would come traipsing out to the stables by herself. He grimaced. He'd only ever known one young lady who would do such a thing, and it was highly unlikely that *that* particular young lady was here. She was engaged to be married, after all. No longer looking for a husband. In fact, she was to be the future Marchioness of Murdock.

Rhys clenched his jaw. He always clenched his jaw when he thought of her. He had to admit, she'd done well for herself. If she couldn't be a duchess, she'd made the next best match, just like the *Times* had reported. A scowl curled Rhys's lip. It made his stomach tighten to think how close he'd come to offering for the beautiful but scheming Lady Julianna Montgomery.

But as disgusted as he was with Lady Julianna, Rhys was even more disgusted with *himself. He'd* been the fool who'd fancied himself falling in love with the chit.

Love? Ha. He'd known his entire life that emotion didn't exist. Hadn't his father told him enough? And yet courting

Julianna all those months ago had made him feel things he'd never felt.

It was a good thing he'd been called away when he had. He'd bloody well been on the verge of offering for her. In fact, it hadn't been until after the accident, after it had all been too late, that his valet had read that fateful copy of the *Times* to him. John had got in the habit of reading him the paper every day. He'd recited the story about the gorgeous Lady Julianna Montgomery and how she'd been forced to set her sights on Murdock, having let the last eligible duke slip through her fingers.

Rhys had nearly vomited that day. He'd given John some excuse for needing to be alone, and he'd nearly wretched into his wash bowl. It had taken him several minutes to pull himself together and steel his resolve. Lady Julianna had been an excellent actress, nothing more, and his own damned desire to be noble and do the right thing for once—a desire she'd inspired in him, ironically—had kept him from offering for her before he left that spring.

And after—*after*—offering for her had been out of the question. Or at least it had been until...recently. But she'd done him a courtesy. She'd gone and betrothed herself to someone else. Well, Murdock could have the actress. Rhys would do quite fine remaining a bachelor.

"Yes, milady," Mr. Hereford's voice rang out from the entrance to the stables. "One of the Arabians be right over there. I'm certain our newest groomsman, Mr. Worthy, will be 'appy ta show 'im ta ye."

Rhys smiled as he brushed the horse's side one last time. Mr. Hereford had obviously raised his voice so Rhys would hear that one of the young ladies from the house party had arrived. Time for his first performance. He just hoped whoever her chaperone was didn't recognize him. At any rate, he could pretend as well as Kendall and Bell. He *refused* to lose the bet.

Rhys cleared his throat, straightened his shoulders, and put on his most charming and devilish smile. The one that was certain to make this young lady swoon. He rounded the back of the horse to come out of the stall and greet her.

The moment he saw her, he felt both the charm and the devilishness slide right off his face. She sauntered toward him in an emerald-green riding habit and dark-brown leather boots, with a crop in her hand. Of all the ladies in the world, what in the bloody hell was Lady Julianna Montgomery doing here? She was no debutante!

CHAPTER FOUR

Julianna stopped walking when the groomsman brought the Arabian toward her. The man's face was hidden on the far side of the impressive horse.

"Here he be," called the stablemaster. "Alabaster."

Julianna allowed her gaze to travel the horse. His high crest, his elegant back, his fine flank, his lovely strong legs, his glorious hooves. "Oh, look at him," she exclaimed, clasping her hands and the crop to her chest. "He is magnificent, isn't he?"

"Yes," came an arrogant, deep, and somewhat familiar-sounding voice from the other side of the horse. "And the horse isn't bad either."

Julianna blinked, then narrowed her eyes. Had she heard the man correctly? Of all the impudent, arrogant, inappropriate things for a groomsman to say. Something about the voice made the skin on the back of her neck tingle, however. She knew that voice.

She swallowed. Hard. Bless it. What in the devil was *he* doing here?

Julianna took a deep reassuring breath just as Rhys

Sheffield stepped out from the other side of the horse. He executed a deep bow. "My lady."

Julianna blinked again. What was this? Why in the world was he dressed as a… a…groomsman? She tilted her head to the side, staring at him as if either he or she had lost their mind. Surely one of them had.

"Lady Julianna," the stablemaster said. "This is Alabaster." He pointed to the horse. "And this is our newest stablehand, Mr. Worthy." He pointed to the man. The stablemaster's eyes darted to and fro and he tugged at his collar, looking quite uncomfortable. Obviously, the man didn't think for a moment that the duke standing next to them was a blessed stablehand. What exactly was going on here?

Julianna was just about to open her mouth to say something about the ludicrousness of it all when Rhys caught her eye, shook his head ever so slightly as if trying to tell her to remain quiet and announced, "A pleasure, my lady. I'm *completely* at your service. Your *slightest* wish is my command."

It was the way that he emphasized the two words that made Julianna's breath catch in her throat, while a tingle of apprehension—dare she think, excitement?—shot down her spine. She snapped her mouth shut. Turning back toward the stablemaster, she searched his face, but all trace of irony had disappeared. Her gaze moved back and forth between the two men, examining them.

She clearly saw the silent plea in Rhys's cobalt-blue eyes, begging her to play along at least for the time being. Something was amiss here. Something significant, but if her instincts weren't mistaken, she was about to be afforded a priceless opportunity: to treat Rhys Sheffield like a servant.

Julianna crossed her arms tightly over her chest. She narrowed her gaze on him and eyed him up and down from the tip of his boots to the top of his head. Damn him. The man was every bit as good looking as he'd been the last time she'd seen him. More so perhaps, with the slightest bit of gray in his black hair and a few new wrinkles at the corners of his eyes. He was just as fit and tall and oh-this-was-not-helpful.

Just what sort of a game was he playing? She didn't trust him. Not for one moment. But her curiosity overcame her frustration. She would play along. For now. Oh, yes, she would. A grin she could not stop spread itself wide across her lips. She cupped a hand behind her ear feigning a hearing problem.

"What was that, my good man?" Meeting Rhys's eyes, she hoped she conveyed the proper amounts of both I'm-going-to-torture-you and I-plan-to-enjoy-it. "Something about my wishes?"

He bowed again. His voice, when it came, had a deep timbre that made her insides quake with some old feeling she did not want to explore. "Your slightest wish, milady, is my command." As he straightened again, she saw an unmistakable sparkle in his eye. And somehow, he'd managed to make the entire sentence sound positively *obscene*.

Oh, he was up to something all right. What was it?

Confound him. He was just as bold and arrogant and confident and oh, he was *everything* he used to be. How had she ever found him attractive? Very well. He was good-looking to be certain, but his manners left much to be desired and she'd never met a man more in love with himself. Detestable!

She would want to slap his handsome face, but that would mean she cared, and she positively did *not* care. Not anymore. She'd made a new match. A better one. Perhaps not with a duke, but with someone who was consistent and true. Someone altogether unlike Rhys Sheffield.

Before Julianna had a chance to reply, the stablemaster

mumbled something under his breath about getting back to his duties and took off in another direction, his coattails flapping behind him.

And just like that, the stablemaster was gone, leaving Julianna standing next to the finest-looking horse and (confound it) the finest-looking man she'd ever seen. For the first time in one year, three months, two weeks, and four days, she was alone with Rhys Sheffield.

CHAPTER FIVE

Rhys had been forced to make a quick decision. Either he could run off and risk forfeiting his bet on the first day—bad-form, that—or he could take his chances and risk Julianna recognizing him. The first choice meant instant failure. The second would at least give him a fighting chance, and he'd always been an admirer of a fighting chance.

He'd held out the slightest hope that Julianna might not recognize him given the way he was dressed, until he'd made that crack about his looks. Blast it. He simply couldn't help himself. She'd given him the perfect opening. Her spine had stiffened. Obviously, she remembered his voice. That was interesting. Or at least it might have been if he gave a toss about her anymore. She also was aware of the Arabians. That was interesting as well, but for an entirely different reason. The lady knew her horses.

He allowed his gaze to take in her form, from the tips of her brown, leather riding boots to the top of her emerald velvet hat that brought out the gorgeous color of her light-green eyes. Eyes he'd once got lost in. Eyes he'd once seen his future in.

The past year certainly hadn't served to diminish her beauty any. She was as lovely as ever. Her pert nose, dusky pink lips, and long lashes. She was tall, willowy, and blond, a work of art. A work of art with a gold-digging heart. Seeing her again physically hurt. Like a punch to the gut. He sucked air through his teeth then pasted on his most disarming smile. There was no reason not to be charming after all. He was known for it. If he wasn't charming it would seem as if —God forbid—he cared.

She probably hated him. For good reason. The feeling was entirely mutual. But there was absolutely no reason not to be cordial to her. Especially now that she obviously had the upper hand. She was holding the key to his winning or losing his bet. And he couldn't afford to lose.

Her voice was low when she spoke. Not exactly a whisper, but low enough to ensure no one would overhear. "It's been a while, *Rhys*, but I could have sworn the last time we spoke, you were a duke." She lifted her chin haughtily.

"And I could have sworn the last time we spoke, you were someone quite different as well; or at least appeared to be."

"What's that supposed to mean?" Her eyes flashed with anger.

He realized immediately he'd made a mistake. Damn. He needed to remain nonchalant and not allow emotion into this exchange. "Oh, nothing."

"So, you're a groomsman now?" she continued, batting her eyelashes at him prettily.

He bit the inside of his cheek to keep from saying, "Yes, and you're still disloyal?" Instead, he said, "Temporarily, yes."

"Care to tell me what you're playing at?" She arched a blond brow at him.

"I'll tell you, milady, in good time, but first, if you don't mind, I'd like to escort you from the stables so we may have privacy in the telling."

She eyed him warily and then glanced at the horse. "Well, I would love to ride Alabaster."

"Of course you would." He gave her a tight smile. "Excuse me while I saddle him again."

Rhys led the horse back to the stall and spent a few minutes putting on the blanket and fastening the girth. He hadn't needed Mr. Hereford's instruction on how to properly saddle a horse. He might be a duke, but he wasn't incompetent when it came to the proper care of horses.

He might not know how to brush out a suit like his valet or serve from the proper bowl like his footmen, but he damn well knew his way around stables. The stables on his father's country estate had been his favorite refuge when he was a boy. They were still his favorite place when he went to Worthington Manor.

As he cinched the girth around Alabaster's middle, Rhys was distracted with thoughts of Julianna. What the bloody hell was she doing here? And why in the bloody hell hadn't Clayton seen fit to tell him that she'd be here? That was more than an oversight. He'd have a few choice words for Clayton when next he saw the man.

Rhys finished preparing the horse with a sidesaddle and brought him back out to where Julianna was standing.

"Where's your mother?" he drawled in as unaffected a tone as he could muster.

"Resting with Mary. I sneaked away."

"That sounds right." He shouldn't condemn her for it. It had been one of the things he'd liked about her when he'd courted her. She wasn't the type of young woman to get all marmish and shy about sneaking off to do things that were

35

more fun than sipping tea and dancing the waltz. Not that they'd ever done anything indecent. Well, save for that time in his study, but that had been over quickly and both of them had remained fully clothed. Mostly.

Rhys came around the side of Alabaster to help Julianna up. He bent low and weaved his fingers together, giving her a step from which to spring. Without demurring, she placed her small booted foot on his hands, and was up in one quick, fluid motion, the horn of the sidesaddle under her knee. She'd always been a good horsewoman, he had to admit reluctantly. That had been another thing he'd liked about her when they were courting.

A whiff of her perfume had struck his nostrils as he'd helped her up. The memory the scent of lilacs evoked made him clench his jaw. It was a bouquet that used to make him hard. This time, it just made him angry.

A few minutes later, he swung himself up on his own mount, a less majestic gelding from Clayton's stable. He motioned for the lady to go ahead of him from the building.

He watched her from behind. An incomparable lady riding an incomparable horse. She sat perfectly straight atop Alabaster. Even Rhys had to admit, they made quite a pair. Meanwhile, he was racking his brain trying to come up with something to tell her about why he was pretending to be a groomsman. He intended to offer her money to keep her silence, of course. He'd use some of the winnings from the bet to pay her off. But he knew her well enough to know that she would ask questions, and he had better be ready with believable answers.

"Would you care to ride to the tree line and back?" he asked as soon as they'd cleared the barn and the fence. The farther they were from the stables, the better the chance of not being overheard. She shouldn't ride out with him, of course, not without a chaperone, but he was not a duke courting a young lady. He was a groomsman escorting a house guest on a ride. It was actually much more acceptable this way.

She shot him a look over her shoulder that clearly indicated she didn't trust him.

"We'll be in full view of the stables the entire way," he offered by way of appeasing her apprehension.

"Very well. I'll see you there." She leaned down, kicked her heel, and set the glorious Arabian off at a fine clip.

Rhys had barely realized that she'd challenged him to a race before she was off. He immediately spurred his own mount into action to catch up. In addition to being a fine horsewoman, she was competitive, too. He remembered that about her. He'd adored that about her. Some would say he was competitive to a fault, and being around Julianna had never bored him the way his time with other young women had.

Whether they'd been playing a card game, skipping stones in a pond in Hyde Park, or racing each other on horseback, Julianna had given as good as she got and never tried to use her sex as a reason for an allowance. She'd managed to beat him a time or two, and that had perhaps been the most thrilling of all. A woman who didn't back down, who was as competitive as he was, and who didn't try to lose in order to assuage his masculinity. Why, he'd never met anyone like her before. Or at least he thought he hadn't until he realized she was only interested in him for his dukedom. She'd probably been acting the entire time. Was she acting now? She no longer had a reason to.

As he galloped along behind her toward the tree line, Rhys couldn't help but admire her form. She rode with confidence and mastered the reins. Her style spoke of years of experience on horses. It had been one of their favorite subjects while he was courting her, to discuss horseflesh.

Blast it. Why did he keep thinking about their courtship? It was history. Water under the proverbial bridge. It meant nothing to him anymore and he bloody well knew it never had meant anything to her, so why was his head filling with all of these memories of a sudden?

Damned if she didn't beat him to the tree line. Although he'd managed to make up a considerable length, she was riding a much finer mount. Of course, a less experienced rider still would have lost to him. He grudgingly had to admit she deserved the win.

"I won," Julianna announced the moment she slowed Alabaster to a soft trot along the fence that ran in front of the trees.

"What did you win?" The devil made him say it. The devil was so often making him say things.

"The race," she replied, a smug look on her face.

"Oh, were we racing?" he asked in the most nonchalant voice he could muster.

"Don't pretend you didn't know it," she said with a sly grin. One that he remembered. One that made him want to look away.

"Very well, you won. What is my forfeit?" There was that devil again. Sneaky bastard.

Julianna's horse came to a stop and she dismounted using the fence posts. She continued to slowly walk Alabaster, while rubbing his flank and gently talking to the beautiful horse. Rhys dismounted too and soon tied both horses to one of the fence posts. Then he turned to face Julianna.

Her green eyes flashed with a mixture of amusement and probably pride. "I'd say your forfeit should be telling me why you've decided to take up a new profession."

Rhys pushed his long hair away from his face with his fingers. He clearly had two choices. He could lie to her or he could tell her the truth. Julianna was clever and shrewd. It would be waste of time to lie to her and try to get her to believe some silly tale about why he was pretending to be a groomsman. No, the most expedient way to get Julianna to help him would obviously be to explain to her what was in it for her.

"I need you to keep the secret," he said. There. A lob across the bow. Just to see her reaction.

Her brow furrowed. "It's a secret that you're pretending to be a groomsman?"

"Well, not to everyone. The other groomsmen and the stablemaster all know."

"What about the coachmen?" she asked with an irrepressible grin.

"*All* the servants are aware," he clarified, placing his hands on his hips.

She crossed her arms over her chest and eyed him warily. "I cannot imagine Lord Clayton doesn't know."

"Of course, he knows," Rhys replied, tilting his head to one side.

"Then who, precisely, are you trying to keep it from?" She put a pretty smile on her face and batted her dark eyelashes again.

"The guests," Rhys announced.

"The guests?" Her eyebrows raised and her countenance dripped with skepticism. "Why the guests?"

He expelled a breath. "It's complicated and it doesn't matter. Let's just say I'll make it worth your while if you play along and don't tell anyone who I am."

"Worth my while?" She narrowed her eyes and took a step toward him. "I must admit. I cannot *wait* to hear what you think would be 'worth my while.'"

Trying to appear as nonchalant as possible, he leaned back against a nearby tree. "Money, of course."

She laughed out loud at that, her arms falling to her sides. "You're offering to *pay* me for my silence?"

He shrugged one shoulder. "You're refusing?"

She pulled the crop between her fingers. "I don't know if I'm refusing or not. First, I'd like to hear why you're pretending to be a groomsman, especially since the others in the stables already know who you are. Did you pay all of them as well?"

Rhys had to smile at that. "No, they are keeping the secret as a favor to their employer, Clayton."

He pushed himself off the tree and grinned at her.

"Very well. Why exactly do you want the other guests to think you're a groomsman?" she asked sweetly, lightly slapping the crop into her gloved palm.

Rhys paced in front of her. She had a way of making the whole thing sound even more ludicrous than it already was. "Does it truly matter?"

Julianna shrugged. "Perhaps not, but you're requesting my help, so I feel as if I have the right to know."

He braced a hand on the fence post. "How much do you want?" The words came out much more harshly than he'd meant them to.

She arched a brow. "How much are you willing to pay?"

"Don't play coy, Julianna. It doesn't suit you. How much money will it take for you to keep your silence? To pretend you never saw me? To act as if I'm just a groomsman named Mr. Worthy for the remainder of the house party?"

She moved back toward Alabaster and rubbed his flank. "You're actually serious, aren't you?"

Rhys tossed a hand in the air. "Of course, I'm serious." Damn it. He was letting her spark his temper. He needed to take a deep breath.

She turned to look at him, eyes wide. "You truly believe you can *pay* me for my silence?"

"Is there something else you'd prefer to money?" he drawled, hands back on his hips. His patience was quickly growing short.

A sly smile curved her perfect lips. "Oh, yes, actually, there is."

CHAPTER SIX

At the dinner table that evening, Julianna sat between her mother and sister and could think of little else than her conversation with Worthington at the tree line that afternoon. If anyone had told her a sennight ago that she would have had the most insane discussion today with Rhys Sheffield of all people, she scarcely would have believed it.

But now she pushed the roasted goose around her plate, completely without appetite, unable to think about anything other than what the devil Worthington was doing out in the stables pretending to be a groomsman.

The man had had the audacity to offer her money. She could *almost* laugh again. As if money was what she wanted from him. Hardly. She didn't need money. She wanted for nothing. Her father was wealthy, and she was about to marry one of the richest men in the *ton*. No. No. She didn't want *money* from Rhys Sheffield.

She wanted…revenge.

Of course, she hadn't blurted that out to him. She wasn't witless. She had told him she would keep his secret for the price of him telling her exactly why he was pretending to be a groomsman. And she made it clear that nothing but the absolute truth would do. She was fully confident in her ability to discern whether he was telling the truth. For two reasons. One, she'd always been good at reading people and two, he wasn't a particularly adept liar.

He'd been none too pleased with that request. He'd offered her an exorbitant amount of money for her silence instead. But that offer merely served to inform her that he was desperate to keep his secret, which made her all the more interested in learning it. Money meant little to her. Revenge meant everything. Revenge on the man who had broken her heart into a thousand little pieces. *That* was without price. And if she could learn why he was pretending to be a servant, she just might be able to thwart his purposes and thereby exact her revenge. Revenge that had been long in coming.

Julianna stared absently at the portrait of Lady Clayton that hung above the fireplace in the dining room as her mind drifted back to many months ago. The last time she'd seen Rhys.

It had been an unseasonably cool May night when she'd stolen out of the Cranberrys' ball to meet Rhys on the veranda. She was wearing a violet-colored gown with a high waist, and tiny flowers embroidered along the sleeves and hem. During their dance earlier, Rhys had asked her to meet him here and time seemed to move with infinite slowness during the hour she'd been forced to wait.

She rushed out into the cool air, nearly breathless with anticipation. Rhys had been standing there, near the balustrade. One hand in his waistcoat pocket. He was wearing black superfine evening attire with a snowy white cravat. His black hair had been slicked back and his dark-blue eyes twinkled in the moonlight. He looked so handsome she'd wanted to hurtle herself into his arms. Instead, she forced herself to slow her pace and make her way toward him gracefully. Thankfully, they were alone.

"Rhys," she'd breathed as he took her hands in his and pulled her close.

"Julianna," he'd answered, resting a hand possessively on her hip.

They'd begun calling each other by their Christian names ever since the night she'd sneaked into Rhys study during a dinner party and he'd found her there. She had hurtled herself into his arms that night, and Rhys had had to be the one to break off their encounter before it went too far.

"I'm glad I have the chance to see you before I go," he breathed.

A frown covered Julianna's face. "Go?" She shook her head. Where was he going? Why?

"Yes, unfortunately, I must go to the country tomorrow to...visit my mother." His hand fell away from her hip.

"I see," Julianna answered. She was disappointed to hear that he was leaving, but surely, he wouldn't stay away long.

"I promise to return as quickly as possible," he said, sincerity in his eyes.

She opened her little violet satin reticule and took out a handkerchief. One she'd sprayed with the lilac water she used as perfume. "Take this," she said, handing him the handkerchief. "To remember me."

He'd taken the slip of fabric from her hand and squeezed it tightly before putting it to his nose and then tucking it inside his coat pocket. "Julianna, sweet Julianna, how could I ever forget you?"

❧

THOSE HAD BEEN the last words he'd said to her. He'd touched her cheek and let his gaze rove over her face as if he was studying her to remember. He'd left her moments later, standing on the balcony alone.

She'd had no clue that he'd had no intention of coming back. He'd let her believe like a fool and he'd even taken her blessed handkerchief as if he had any intention of keeping it to remember her by. God, he'd been a rogue, a scoundrel. Detestable.

A sennight had passed and then a fortnight. She'd done her best to keep up her happy carefree *façade* in public, but the longer he was gone with no word, the more difficult it was for her to believe he was ever coming back.

Finally, after the Season had ended and she and her family had left for her father's country house, she'd received a letter from Worthington. It was poorly written and vague. Its contents were completely inconsistent with how he'd acted the last time she saw him.

He wrote some asinine thing about how he hoped she hadn't thought more of their acquaintance than he had. Lies, all of it. Hurtful lies. But she'd vowed to never let him see her pain.

Fine. Perhaps she'd looked for him the following Season. Perhaps she'd kept an eye out at every single *ton* event she attended. But he hadn't returned. It was as if he'd disappeared. In fact, she hadn't laid eyes on him again until this afternoon in Clayton's stables.

Yes, the Duke of Worthington had hurt her, deeply, and she intended to inflict the same amount of damage on him. If she could learn why Rhys was pretending to be a groomsman, she'd have the upper hand in this entire situation and could use it—would use it—to her advantage. He obviously meant to continue to pretend he was a groomsman. She'd already thought of half a dozen ways she could torture him. What was better than revenge that was fun at the same time?

This afternoon, they'd been interrupted by one of the other groomsmen riding out to inform them another one of the guests wanted to see Alabaster. But Rhys had managed to whisper to her to meet him in the same location at the same time tomorrow and he would give her his answer. His answer regarding whether he would tell her the truth about whatever game he was playing. The way Julianna saw it, the man had little choice but to tell her the truth. Money wasn't about to sway her. Only the truth would do.

She glanced around the dining room. It was full of guests talking and laughing, but for some reason she felt as if she was all alone. Where was Rhys at the moment? Out in the stables? Was he sleeping on a pile of hay? She nearly snorted at that thought. Surely, he wasn't spending the nights out there. Or was he? She supposed it depended on exactly what he was up to. Wherever he was, she hoped he was completely unsettled, and *she* was the one who had unsettled him. Turn-about was fair play after all.

Mary said something to her that she didn't hear, and Julianna did her best to smile and nod. She glanced around at all of the young ladies at the table. They were all here for the same purpose. To find a husband. It hadn't escaped her notice that the guest list seemed to be comprised almost entirely of young ladies who had made their debuts this past Season and who were still not betrothed. Of course, her darling Mary was one of them.

It also hadn't escaped Julianna's notice that the guest list seemed to be sorely lacking in eligible males. Given that, and the fact that one of the nation's most notorious dukes was gallivanting around the stables pretending to be a grooms-man, Julianna was convinced this was no ordinary house party. It was no ordinary house party at all.

Her perusal of the table turned up Miss Frances Wharton. Julianna had met the young woman briefly at one of the events of the past Season, but they hadn't had much of a chance to speak. Tonight, the poor lady looked bored to tears listening to Sir Reginald Francis drone on and on about his friendship with the Prince Regent. Sir Reginald could be a complete drain on one's nerves. She hoped, for Miss Wharton's sake, that Sir Reginald wasn't considering offering for her.

Apart from her proximity to the knight, Julianna had a flash of envy for Miss Wharton. It had to be somewhat freeing to simply be a normal young woman. She and Mary had been raised to be anything but normal. Since the day she was born, at least as far back as she could remember, Julianna was marked for greatness (her mother's words).

For the daughter of a duke, greatness meant ensuring she made the most advantageous match with the most eligible partner possible. Was it terribly simple to be Miss Wharton? Just a pretty girl with a normal family. Instead of an 'incomparable'—Julianna hated that word— with the largest dowry and best connections, expected to make the best match.

Julianna expelled her breath. She'd never been at liberty to simply speak to a gentleman, decide if she actually enjoyed his company. God forbid. No, she'd been pointed in the direction of the most eligible man in any room and told to use her looks and manners to entice him. Her entire life, all anyone ever said to her was how pretty she was. All anyone ever thought she wanted to talk about was what sort of a match she would make once she came of age.

When she'd met Rhys, yes, he'd been the most eligible man in the room. He was powerful and titled and handsome, but she'd actually enjoyed his company. She'd actually believed for one short, sweet bit of time that she'd found love in addition to fulfilling her duty.

That's what had made his betrayal all the more painful to bear. She'd been foolishly falling in love with him, while he'd merely been playing a game with her. The same game he no doubt played with every Season's crop of debutantes. The man was cruel, pure and simple.

Julianna stopped pushing the goose around the plate and set down her fork and knife. She no longer had it in her to pretend she was hungry. Her lack of appetite had little to do with her dinner companions and everything to do with the fact that she would be confronting Worthington again tomorrow and was certain to come away the winner.

A smile curled her lips as she allowed a footman to remove her still-full plate. She glanced up just as the footman pulled the plate to his chest.

Wait just a moment! Was that the Earl of Kendall dressed as a footman?

CHAPTER SEVEN

W as she coming? Rhys kicked at the dirt near the fence with his boot and paced back and forth for the dozenth time. If so, she was certainly taking her time. He should have known better than to trust Julianna Montgomery. Why, for all he knew, she was back in the house regaling all the other young ladies with the scandalous news that the Duke of Worthington was out in the stables, pretending to be a groomsman.

After a fitful night's sleep, Rhys had spoken to Clayton this morning in the library when he'd met all his friends to discuss their first day as servants. Clayton had given him some excuse about not knowing until the last minute that the Duchess of Montlake and her daughter Mary were bringing Julianna with them. Rhys supposed that stood to reason.

Still pacing, he slapped his gloves against his leg so hard he was certain it would leave a welt.

Damn it. If she didn't arrive, he would be forced to face his friends and the fact that he lost the bet due to ill-timing and an unfortunate last-minute addition to the guest list.

The sound of galloping caught his attention and he

swiveled to see Julianna riding hell-for-leather across the meadow toward him. Her cheeks were red with her effort and she had an enormous smile on her face. Still clutching his gloves in his fist, he crossed his arms over his chest and glared at her as she approached. No doubt she was looking forward to telling him she'd already sounded the alarm.

She came to a stop near him, dismounted quickly and effortlessly, and threw him the reins.

"You're the groomsman, aren't you?" she asked with a coy smile when he gave her a surprised look in reply.

Rhys took the reins and tied the horse to the fence near his own mount. Then he crossed his arms over his chest again and stared down his nose at her. "Well?"

"Well, what?" She stared right back at him. Today she was wearing a sapphire blue riding habit and had a perfectly unrepentant look of delight on her face. "I thought I came here for you to tell me what you'd decided."

Rhys frowned. "What I decided about what?"

She pursed her lips. "Oh, come now, you're older than I am, but you're not *that* old. You told me yesterday you needed to decide whether you're willing to tell me the truth."

"First of all, you're right, I'm *not* that old, and secondly, I don't think I have much choice other than to tell you the truth. You said you don't want money. Have you changed your mind?"

If it was possible for the smile on Julianna's face to widen, it did. "No. I haven't changed my mind. I don't want money. I want you to tell me why you're sneaking around Clayton's stables pretending to be a groomsman."

"Blast it. Isn't there *some* amount of money you need?" he grumbled.

She gave him a tight smile. "No. You cannot buy me off, Rhys." Her voice was firm and deliberate.

Rhys cursed under his breath again. "Fine. If I tell you,

you must promise—no, *swear*—not to tell any of the other guests. Including your mother and sister."

"I promise." She gave him a beatific smile.

"Fine." Damn it. He didn't entirely trust her, but he had little choice. He paced away and then abruptly turned to face her again. "The truth is that I've made a bet with my friends."

Her brows shot up. "Really?" She shook her head. "I should have guessed."

"Too late to ask for money now." The look he gave her dripped with sarcasm.

She rolled her eyes. "Who did you make this bet with?"

"Clayton, Kendall, and Bellingham."

"Kendall, eh?" The hint of a smile curled the corner of her lips.

Rhys scratched at the back of his neck. "It was sort of Kendall's idea," he admitted.

A gleam came into Julianna's eyes. "Is *that* why he was parading around the dining table last night pretending to be a footman?"

Rhys's eyes widened and he gave a start. "You saw him?"

"Of course I saw him. I'm not blind. What I want to know is what in heaven's name are you two up to?"

Rhys shook his head and searched her face for the truth. "Did you say anything? Did you tell anyone?"

Julianna crossed her arms over her chest. "Of course not. I'm far too interested in learning why the two of you are trying to pretend to be servants."

"The *three* of us," Rhys replied with a sigh. He might as well out with the entire plot. She already knew too much.

"Bellingham's doing it, too?" She arched a brow.

"Yes," Rhys replied. "He's valeting Lord Copperpot."

She rolled her eyes again. "Of course he is. Very well, go ahead," she continued with a nod. "Tell me why the three of you are pretending to be servants."

Rhys pushed his hair back with one hand. "If you must know, we bet each other a goodly sum that we each couldn't pass as servants for the duration of this house party."

"A fortnight?" she breathed. "That's a lofty goal indeed."

"Perhaps."

"Without being found out, you mean?" she asked.

He nodded. "Yes, that's part of it."

"What's the other part?" Her eyes remained narrowed on him as if she didn't believe he was telling the truth.

"We must be convincing and actually perform duties as servants. The guests mustn't discover who we really are."

She pressed her lips together briefly. "But you haven't lost yet even though I know?"

"That's correct. We expected there to be at least one or two people who'd recognize us and who we'd have to take into confidence."

She looked positively delighted. "Am I the first?"

"To my knowledge. And hopefully the last," he nearly growled.

"Oh, come now, Rhys, you didn't truly believe you'd all be able to pass as servants and have no one recognize you, did you?"

When he didn't answer, she paused for a moment in thought and then said, "Allow me to guess. You all came up with this idea while drinking."

The disgruntled look on his face must have told her she was right. She laughed out loud. "You did, didn't you? You were intoxicated and came up with this scheme. However did you manage to convince Clayton and his lady?"

Rhys pinched the bridge of his nose. His head was throbbing. How had he managed to get himself into this situation? "Clayton was with us. How he convinced Thea, I'm blissfully unaware."

"And you're all doing it?" she asked.

52

"Well, not Clayton, of course. We needed someone to play host."

Julianna shook her head. "How did you ever think you'd manage it? Kendall was standing in the dining room for all to see."

Rhys tilted his head to the side. "Did anyone else recognize him?"

"Not that I noticed," Julianna replied, "I kept glancing around, expecting others to realize who he was, but no one did."

"Yes, that was Bellingham's point. Servants are often overlooked by those whom they serve."

Julianna appeared to quietly contemplate that thought for a moment. "I noticed you right away," she finally said. Was it his imagination or had her voice caught?

"I'm noticeable," he replied with an unrepentant grin.

She pursed her lips. "I see you're also still arrogant."

"*Confident* is the word I prefer. And I'm quite serious, one of the reasons Clayton stuck me in the stables is so that I would be less noticeable."

"Let me guess, the other reason he stuck you in the stables is because he was entirely certain you would never be able to perform the duties of either a competent footman or a decent valet?" She finished with an undaunted smile.

Rhys narrowed his eyes on her. Whatever else he disliked about her, she was astute. She'd been able to guess a great deal about their plan and the details surrounding it. He could only hope she was trustworthy. At least when it came to this. Because he had no other choice but to trust her to keep her word.

She tapped her cheek with the tip of the crop. "The guest list makes sense now, I suppose. Most of the guests are debutantes and their mothers. Chosen to ensure the majority of them wouldn't know any of you, I presume."

"Precisely."

"I think you're all mad," she said, turning and walking back toward her mount. "I also think there's no possibility you won't be found out."

Rhys blew out a deep breath. "Be that as it may, I've told you the truth. Will you promise to keep the secret for all three of us?"

"I've already promised," Julianna replied, using the fence post to hoist herself easily upon her horse's back.

Rhys breathed a sigh of relief. "Thank you." He let his chin fall to his chest momentarily. He was getting off easily. She'd promised to keep the secret and he could keep his winnings. Dare he hope she was actually a bit decent after all?

Julianna gathered the reins and turned the horse to face him. "I promised to keep your secret," she said. "I never promised not to enjoy every moment of watching you try to pass yourself off as a servant. Including ordering you about myself."

CHAPTER EIGHT

S he was already having fun and she'd barely even begun. After Rhys accompanied Julianna back to the stables, she immediately began peppering him with demands to perform a variety of chores.

"Violet needs a rub down," she pointed out, gesturing to her beloved horse that she'd brought with her.

"As you wish, my lady," Rhys said, bowing. He left momentarily and returned carrying two buckets of water. One he placed in front of Violet to drink, the other he used with a sponge to rub down the horse. He talked quietly to Violet in soothing tones as he did so.

Julianna found herself wishing very much that she knew what he was saying to the mare. It sounded kinder than anything he'd said to *her* since he'd seen her yesterday. He finished by softly brushing Violet, including her lovely dark mane. He was adept with horses, she would give him that.

When he was finished, he stood to the side, bowed and said, "What do you think, my lady?"

Julianna thought she'd never wished so much to be a

horse, but she was not about to say that out loud. Instead she lifted her chin and said, "Now Violet's stall needs mucking."

He arched a brow, then glanced down at the hay in the stall. "It looks clean to me, my lady. I mucked it this morning actually."

She scoffed at that, highly doubting he knew how to muck a stall. She would challenge him to prove his boast was true. "Be that as it may, I'd like it mucked again, please." She did her best to sound imperious.

Julianna watched from several paces away as Rhys pushed a wheelbarrow over to Violet's stall, gathered a pitchfork from somewhere in the recesses of the stable, and set to his task with an enthusiasm she found quite surprising.

After only a few minutes, sweat dripped from his brow and his shirt became plastered to his broad chest, outlining his muscles and flat abdomen. Julianna plucked at the neckline of her riding habit. It was unseasonably warm today, wasn't it?

Rhys didn't stop, nor did he look up. He pitched fork after fork of hay into the barrow. The stall was cleaned in under a quarter of an hour. And perhaps most astonishing of all, he'd done it all with nary a complaint. He wheeled the dirty contents to another part of the stables, returning with a wheelbarrow full of fresh hay, which he then proceeded to dump into Violet's stall and spread in a thick, clean layer using the pitchfork again.

When he was finished, he propped up the pitchfork and rested a gloved hand atop it. "Is it to your liking, my lady?" he asked in his most congenial tone.

Julianna had to pick up her jaw from the stable floors before she could answer. She marched toward the stall, haughtily lifting her nose, and examined his work as if she were the stablemaster herself. "It'll do," she replied, secretly thinking he'd done a better job than the groomsmen in her own stables.

She didn't have long to examine his handiwork, however, before she had to invent his next task. She might have been impressed by his ability to muck the stall so thoroughly, but he'd only completed two chores, after all. She intended to make it her daily occupation to get him to quit and forfeit his bet. She suspected it would take several more chores before he'd be willing to give up the bet that seemed so important to him.

"Violet needs to be fed," she blurted next.

"With pleasure, milady," he replied, bowing.

"What was that?" She cupped a hand behind her ear. Oh, she did adore it when he called her milady. She loved to make him repeat it. She was certain the other servants in the stable were convinced she was hard of hearing, but she didn't care one whit. It was priceless to make Rhys Sheffield bow to her, and she intended to enjoy every single moment of it.

Without saying another word, Rhys left with the wheelbarrow again, this time returning with more hay and a bag of grain. He quickly set to work filling Violet's trough.

What Julianna hadn't counted on, however, was that he would spread the hay with his shirt off. He egregiously pulled the garment over his head with both hands and tossed it atop the stall door. She was forced to watch the man's muscles flexing under a fine coat of perspiration. Her mouth went dry.

Rhys's body looked as if it had been sculpted by a master. And having to stare at him from the other side of the stall while he worked was downright disruptive to her thoughts. It irked her. He was doing it just to be detestable. She knew it.

Very well. He *was* detestable. She'd never said he was bad looking. In fact, his looks were the least objectionable thing about him. Though she'd die before she admitted that out loud to another living soul.

The sight of his gleaming muscles made her pull out her handkerchief and blot her forehead. Her temper shortened considerably while he remained shirtless.

"Too much grain," she snapped.

He bowed.

"Too much hay," she announced.

He bowed again.

"That bit of hay looks dirty," was next.

He left and retrieved an entirely new bale of hay that was pristine, which he pitched shirtless again. Julianna had to turn around and pretend to examine the tack wall in order to get a reprieve from staring at his muscles.

"What next, milady?" His voice made her turn back around.

What next? *What next?* "Violet would like an apple, Mr. Worthy. Would you feed her one? With your shirt *on*, if you please."

His grin was downright roguish. He knew he'd affected her. She could tell by the arrogant look on his face. "It would be my *pleasure*, my lady," Rhys replied, smiling at her mostly charmingly before retreating to a back room of the stables. He returned moments later wearing a clean shirt and carrying two apples in his hand.

He bowed again. "I thought perhaps you might like an apple as well, my lady."

She arched a brow. "A horse's apple?"

"It's just an apple." He lowered his voice. "But perhaps you'd like me to *feed* it to you."

She smirked. That proved it. Her orders had got to him. Good. "Don't put it past me," she whispered back.

One of the other groomsmen walked past. The man doffed his hat and grinned at Rhys. "Good day, Mr. Worthy."

Julianna squinted at the man. Was it her imagination or did the servant actually seem *pleased* to see Worthington?

"Good day, Oswald," Rhys called back, waving at the man. "How's your tooth?"

Oswald rubbed his jaw. "It's right as rain ever since I mixed up that poultice ye recommended."

"Be certain to use it the rest of the week," Rhys replied. "Even if your tooth's feeling better."

"I certainly will, Yer Gr—" Oswald had a choking fit for a few moments before clearing his throat and saying. "I, certainly will, er, *Mr. Worthy.*"

The man continued on his way and Julianna plunked her hands on her hips and shook her head at Rhys. None of the servants were doing a particularly good job of remembering to call him 'Mr. Worthy.' She wondered if they knew she was already aware of his true identity.

"Are you paying them, too?" she asked Rhys after Oswald had disappeared.

Rhys cocked his head to the side and grinned. "Not a farthing."

"You're not even paying them to pretend they like you?" she countered.

Rhys gave her a mock-hurt look. Then his countenance turned serious. "No, unlike some young ladies, they aren't interested in my money over my friendship."

Julianna leaned back, aghast. "What the devil do you mean by that?"

"Isn't it obvious?" he replied, his voice full of scorn.

She blinked. Of course, it was obvious. He clearly believed *she* had been friendly to him in the past due to his money. But nothing could have been further from the truth.

Detestable honestly had the gall to act as if she'd been the one to wrong *him*? "The only thing obvious to me is that arrogant men apparently need to prove to the world that they can woo women whom they don't actually want."

Rhys opened his mouth to retort when another one of the stablehands came bounding up to him.

"Mr. Worthy, Mr. Worthy," the young man said, doffing his hat and bowing to Julianna. "I did what ye said when training that mare this mornin', and wouldn't ye know it, she took to it right away. No longer refuses to follow me around the paddock on the lead."

"Excellent," Rhys replied, grinning at the boy. "I'm glad to hear it, Martin. Keep up the good work."

Grinning from ear to ear, the boy quickly left, and Julianna turned to stare at Rhys, eyeing him with a mixture of suspicion and surprise.

"What?" Rhys asked, clearly noticing her attention.

"I just...I suppose I never realized how...good you are... with people. I have to admit you have a knack with both horses and men."

A grin spread across his face, displaying his perfect white teeth. "Why, Lady Julianna, is that a compliment?"

She shrugged. "I suppose so."

"I'll choose to believe you truly mean it," he said with a chuckle.

She crossed her arms over her chest. There it was again, the implication that she had been a false friend, or at least had given him false flattery in the past. It was so like Rhys to think *he* was the wronged party in their falling out. *She* was the one who had every reason to be hurt and dislike him, not the other way around. She refused to let him twist what had happened between them.

Finally, he walked to the stall wall, folded his arms atop it, leaned over and said, "What else can I do for you, my lady?"

Julianna had to admit he'd taken it in stride while she snapped orders at him all morning. He'd even managed to keep a perfectly calm look on his face as he carried out each of her demands. But he was a coddled aristocrat, not a stablehand. There had to be a way to spark his temper. If only she could get him to fly off the handle. Especially when Mr. Hereford was in the vicinity.

At the moment, however, she was hot, tired, and frustrated. She needed a meal and a chance to think. Not to mention Mama was probably looking for her by now. Julianna needed to formulate her plot more precisely. She would return to the stables and break him. She simply needed time.

"I'm going back to the house now, Mr. Worthy," she said, giving him a tight smile.

"So soon, my lady?" he said, his smile as-fake-as-you-please.

She narrowed her eyes on him. "Don't worry. I'll be back." She hoped it sounded like the threat it was.

"I cannot wait," he drawled.

She batted her eyelashes at him prettily. "In fact, I'll be back tomorrow morning. I'd like you to take my sister and me on a ride to the lake." She paused and her smile intensified. "Right after dawn."

His perfectly charming *façade* crumbled momentarily before he replaced it with a wide smile. He hated early mornings. He'd told her that once.

"I look forward to it, milady." His smile was nearly angelic. She hoped it pained him to be so false.

Moments later, as Julianna walked back to the manor house, a smile curled her lips. She may not have made him quit yet, but she honestly couldn't recall the last time she'd had so much fun. Right up until the time he'd implied she'd lied and played him false at least. *That* was maddening.

Though she had to admit today had been full of surprises. Not only had Rhys not quit, he hadn't even balked at the chores she'd asked him to perform. In fact, he'd done them all with something that resembled aplomb. She was almost... impressed. Who knew? Apparently, the Duke of Worthington could work hard when necessary.

Not only that, but he was charming—not just to young women, as she'd learned to her own detriment last year, but his charm apparently extended to servants as well. They had either greeted him and seemed to genuinely like him or had gone so far as to come looking for him to thank him for his assistance. It truly boggled the mind.

Very well. The servants liked him. Perhaps it was because they were amused with his playacting as if he were one of them. She refused to allow his seeming friendliness to Clayton's stablehands to make her forget the *months* of torture she'd lived through, wondering if he would return from the country, and *months* of sadness she'd endured after he'd sent her that awful letter.

There. That was the memory she needed to recall the next time Rhys Sheffield seemed truly likable. The man might be slightly charming and able to perform a few tasks in a stable when called upon, but she wasn't about to admit defeat. Besides, anyone could endure one morning of work. She would just have to ensure she made things worse for him tomorrow. Much worse.

CHAPTER NINE

Rhys heaved himself onto his side on the small hay-filled mattress. He was sleeping. Or, more correctly, *attempting* to sleep in his berth above the stables. His head was pounding, and it was deuced uncomfortable, but he had no one to blame for his current accommodations but himself. He'd been the one who'd insisted upon sleeping out here with the other stablehands.

Kendall was sleeping on the fourth floor of the manor house with the other footmen. Bell was there too. At least they had beds. All he had was this mat on the floor. But Rhys wasn't about to allow them to say he'd had the upper hand in winning the bet by accepting better sleeping arrangements.

The hay-filled mat might be a far cry from the downy plushness of the feather-filled mattresses he usually slept upon, but he would make do. Even if tonight's mattress smelled like a horse's arse and bits of hay were sticking into every conceivable part of him.

But the discomfort wasn't what kept him awake. At least not the physical discomfort. No. He was awake because he couldn't stop thinking about Julianna. She'd agreed to keep his secret, but he should have known she had a reason for doing so. Money hadn't interested her. He suspected she was out for revenge. And that's what bothered him. Not that she thought she could get him to quit and forfeit his bet, but that *she* apparently felt as if she were the wronged party in what had happened between them last year.

She was not only title-obsessed, she was also completely mad if she thought he was truly in the wrong. Yes, he'd essentially tossed her over, but he had every reason to do so. It just showed how entitled she was for thinking that of the two of them, *he* was in the wrong.

He flipped over on his back and expelled his breath. There was no use fighting it. He wasn't going to get much sleep tonight. Dawn was probably only a few hours off. No doubt, Julianna had picked dawn just to torture him. He grimaced. He seemed to remember mentioning to her that he and early mornings had never been friends. But one early morning wasn't about to stop him. He could take anything she threw at him. He refused to give her the satisfaction of making him quit.

And it wasn't just her. His friends, too, had ribbed him about being unable to stand the hard work of being a servant. It riled him that no one seemed to believe he was worth a damn other than apparently to be a drunken, gambling lout who just happened to have a duke's title hanging about his neck. Hadn't that always been what the papers reported? Hadn't it always secretly pleased him to make them think they were right? Why was it bothering him now, then?

The worst part was that he should have known better than to believe Julianna had loved him. His father's words thundered in his head, making his head ache worse. *"Women are nothing more than diversions. Pleasant diversion. At times. But don't confuse lust for love. That's a fool's mistake. When it comes time to pick a bride, choose her based on her family pedigree and nothing else. Lust is for mistresses."*

Rhys had been fourteen years old when his father had shared that particular bit of wisdom with him. Years of similar conversations had followed. His father had continued dispensing his advice right up until his last breath. Rhys, at twenty-six, had sat next to the old man's deathbed, dry-eyed and stoic while his father shared his parting advice. "When it comes time to take a bride, my son, it will be the most important business decision of your life. Do not make a mistake."

And Rhys thought he hadn't. He'd actually fallen for Julianna's lies and flirting. But she'd been ready to toss him over at a moment's notice. And if there was one thing he abhorred, it was a woman who was only out for money and title. Loyalty was of the utmost importance. He would stand for nothing less than a loyal wife.

Kendall's experience with Lady Emily had affected him greatly. Kendall had truly loved Lady Emily, all of his friends knew it. The damn sop was head over heels for the chit and she'd written to him days before their wedding and told him she'd received a better offer and was leaving him. She bloody well had expected him to understand, for the love of God. Kendall's heart had been broken.

But when Rhys had heard the news, his heart had hardened. If anyone deserved better, it was Kendall. And now the bloody fool was forced to dress up and playact to find a true bride. It was ludicrous.

Perhaps Rhys would have his solicitor choose his wife for him. At least he wouldn't have to pretend to care, and neither would she. Though he had years left to enjoy himself before he took that irreversible step.

That was another thing that angered him when he thought about how close he'd come to tying the parson's noose around his own neck with Julianna. He'd actually considered marriage at the age of eight and twenty. It was true that he'd had quite a scare last year, but he'd somehow come through it remarkably. He'd been raised to think that fifty would be a more appropriate age to consider fathering his heir. The dukes of Worthington were all long-lived and the last three had produced their heirs past their own middle age. Rhys had every intention of following suit. That is until he'd met Lady Julianna and she'd turned his head so thoroughly. She was an actress and he was a fool.

And far from frustrating him and making him want to quit, the chores she'd had him do today had actually made him feel useful for the first time in as long as he could remember.

He tossed again upon the mattress and came down hard on his side, eliciting an *oompf* from his throat. Damn this uncomfortable bed and damn this bet and damn Julianna for appearing and making it that much more difficult for him to win.

But if it was the last thing he did, he refused to let her break him.

CHAPTER TEN

Mary was terribly frightened of horses. Julianna had convinced her to come to the stables by promising her a nice long walk by the lake after they ate their breakfast picnic. Mary adored walks by the lake. In fact, she preferred them to nearly all other things.

Thankfully, during their months of courtship, Rhys had never met Mary. Mary hadn't been of age at the time, so there had been no occasion for them to meet. It wasn't as if Julianna and Rhys had been betrothed, after all.

Mama, however, was certain to notice Rhys if she saw him, and there were few people Mama hated as much as Rhys Sheffield, so Julianna took care not to let Mama know what she and Mary were doing.

Mama was under the impression that her daughters were going for an early morning stroll through the gardens. She'd no idea they were headed off on a breakfast picnic with a groomsman who was none other than the Duke of Worthington. Not that Mama would believe Julianna if she told her. Why, it sounded ridiculous. What Mama didn't know wouldn't hurt her, however. And at the moment, Julianna had a duke to persecute.

She'd decided that her mistake yesterday may have been in giving him tasks to do that he actually enjoyed. He'd chosen not to be a footman on purpose. So, it stood to reason that if she could make him do tasks more in keeping with those of a footman, namely serving and being endlessly polite and helpful, Rhys just might have a worse time of it.

To Julianna's surprise, when she and Mary arrived at the stables, Rhys was not only awake, he was waiting for them with a smile on his face, standing next to a fully outfitted coach and four. Of course, she knew the smile was completely false, but Mary didn't know that. Having Mary there was perfect. Rhys would be forced to keep that smile plastered to his face all morning. He would also have to remain upon his best behavior. After all, Mary was one of the eligible young women for whom he was playing this game. If Mary learned who he was, he would lose the bet.

"Good afternoon, Mr. Worthy," Julianna called as soon as she entered the stables and saw him standing there.

"Good morning, my lady," he called back in reply. "Are you ready for your excursion?"

"Instead of the coach, I'd love to ride Alabaster," Julianna replied, her smile widening. There. Let him set to work immediately having to undo what he'd already done. That would take him no small amount of time, and no doubt frustrate him.

"Oh, no," Mary interjected, shaking her head and looking quite worried, "you promised we'd ride in a conveyance, Anna."

Poor Mary never would have agreed to come if Julianna had mentioned that she'd wanted to ride. "Very well, Mary. We'll ride in the coach," Julianna acquiesced. She didn't want to frighten her sister.

Rhys's smile was downright dazzling as he stepped forward to meet Mary. "And who might this lovely young woman be?"

Julianna stepped forward too. "Mary, this is Mr. Worthy, one of Lord Clayton's groomsman. He's been taking care of Violet and he's agreed to accompany us today." Julianna was acutely aware of the fact that had he not been playacting it would have been highly inappropriate for her to introduce him to her sister, instead of introducing her sister to him.

"A pleasure," Rhys said, bowing over Mary's hand.

"Nice to meet you, Mr. Worthy," Mary answered prettily.

"Don't worry, Lady Mary," Rhys continued. "I've already picked out the perfect carriage for our ride out to the lake."

"Oh, thank goodness," Mary exclaimed, relief covering her pale features. "I cannot imagine riding atop a horse." She shuddered.

Rhys eyed Julianna over her sister's head and Julianna shrugged. "My sister isn't the lover of horses that I am," she offered in way of explanation.

"Not to worry, Lady Mary," Rhys replied. "You'll be safe and comfortable in the carriage."

As Rhys helped first Mary, then Julianna up into the carriage, Julianna had the thought that he'd likely prepared the carriage ahead of time out of fear that she'd critique him the entire time he was putting the horses to. Not a bad strategy, Julianna had to admit. She would have to think ahead more carefully next time.

They were off within a matter of minutes, Ernest, the coachman, at the reins, with Rhys standing on the running board at the back of the small carriage.

As the conveyance bumped along the narrow dirt road on the way out to the lake that sat in the center of Lord Clayton's enormous property, Julianna did her best to concentrate on the gorgeous scenery amid the misty morning, but all she could think about was Rhys. Rhys Sheffield was riding behind her. Rhys Sheffield was going to be there when she emerged from this carriage. She was about to spend the morning with Rhys Sheffield for the second time in as many days. What insanity had transpired in her life to make this happen? It was as if she was living in a dream. No. No. Not a dream—a blessed nightmare.

Well, on one hand it was a nightmare, while on the other, it was as if Providence was smiling down upon her. After all these months of recrimination, she had Rhys Sheffield precisely where she wanted him. At her mercy. So, why wasn't she thinking of ways to make him pay once they reached the lake, instead of squeezing her handkerchief and entertaining memories about Detestable?

A QUARTER OF AN HOUR LATER, when the small carriage pulled to a stop near the lake, Julianna refused to acknowledge the butterflies that scattered in her middle as Rhys wrenched open the door from the outside.

Mary put a hand to Julianna's sleeve. Her brow was wrinkled with concern. "Are you quite all right, Anna?"

"Yes, why?" Julianna managed past lips that were trembling.

"You don't seem yourself this morning," Mary replied. "You look a bit pale."

"I'm fine." Julianna swallowed and pasted her own fake smile to her lips. She felt as if she were about to face a firing squad instead of the man she'd once (nearly) been betrothed to. But she forced herself to square her shoulders and take a deep breath. She absolutely *refused* to allow him to see her weakness. She would win this battle if it were the last thing she did.

"I do hope the ride wasn't too bumpy," Rhys said, through his ubiquitous charming smile the moment the door was open.

"Not at all, Mr. Worthy," Mary replied, smiling at him sweetly and allowing him to help her down onto the grass.

Lord Clayton's cook had provided Julianna with a picnic basket, and before facing Rhys, she pulled out the basket and a blanket she'd brought with her. Rhys took the items from her and set them into the grass near Mary's feet before turning back to Julianna and offering her his arm.

She reached out and placed her gloved hand on his strong, warm forearm. She nearly gulped when she felt the size of his muscles. Memories flooded back to her. One specific memory: of her lying beneath him on the chaise in his study one night, his hips grinding into hers, his mouth on her neck, her arms around his wide shoulders, pulling him closer, and—

"Are you all right, Julianna?" Mary asked again.

Julianna didn't have to wonder why her sister had asked that time. Heat was burning her cheeks. No doubt she was a bright shade of red. Oh, bless it. Why did she have to have such a vivid memory and why did it have to somehow be triggered every time she touched Rhys Sheffield? Or caught a whiff of his expensive cologne that he apparently was still wearing even while pretending to be a groomsman. Unless... he somehow knew it drove her mad. No, he couldn't know that. Could he?

"I'm...fine," she managed, nearly jumping to the ground in an effort to step away from Rhys, his muscles, and his memory as quickly as possible.

The moment her hand flew away from his sleeve, Rhys bent to pick up the blanket and the picnic basket. "Where would you like me to set up the picnic, milady?" he asked in an overly helpful voice.

Julianna nodded toward the edge of the lake. "Over there will be qu...quite fine."

"Oh, yes, let's sit by the water," Mary said, clasping her hands together and moving ahead of them to find the perfect spot.

Rhys allowed Julianna to lead the way, while Ernest remained at the coach. She could feel Rhys's eyes on her backside. She could only hope he hadn't guessed that she was blushing as a result of touching him. But then again, the man did have enormous confidence, he was probably quite certain she was blushing over him.

Mary stood spinning in a circle in the spot she'd picked, and Rhys set the basket aside and tossed the blanket onto the soft, green grass. Then he set about ensuring all four corners were pulled wide before he picked up the basket, leaned over, and set it on the center of the blanket.

"Would you care for me to serve you?" he asked in a completely nonchalant voice.

"Yes, please," Julianna replied, forcing herself to remain committed to her plan. She'd meant to make Rhys cater to her every whim, but now that he was doing it, why did it feel awkward and uncomfortable? She should be enjoying every moment of this instead of feeling vaguely guilty.

"As you wish, milady," Rhys replied, nodding and bowing.

There, that was more like it. In addition to *milady*, she loved it when he said *as you wish*. She shook her head as if to divest it of the unhelpful thoughts from earlier and set about enjoying herself as Rhys pulled out the contents of the picnic basket. There were two plates and two cloth napkins, two forks, a teapot with still-hot tea inside, two cups and two saucers, a basket of buns, a variety of jams and marmalades, two knives with which to spread the jams, a small basket of boiled eggs, and a small bowl of purple grapes.

Rhys arranged the entire set in a small circle in the center of the blanket, then he removed the basket and set it off to the side on the grass. If he was irked over having to serve as a footman, he showed no signs of it. Bless it.

"This looks delightful," Mary exclaimed.

"It does," Julianna agreed quietly, not meeting Rhys's gaze.

"If there's nothing else, I'll just leave you to it," Rhys said, standing and moving back toward the coach.

"Thank you, Mr. Worthy," Mary said, picking up a knife and dunking it into the jam.

Julianna tried to concentrate on the picnic, but she couldn't help but wonder what Rhys was doing back at the coach. She kept glancing toward the conveyance. At first, he set about giving the horses some water, but soon after he disappeared around the far side of the vehicle and she had no idea what he was doing. Ernest had disappeared too. She sat picking at her bun and wondering.

"What do you think Mr. Worthy and the coachman are doing?" The question from Mary had been so exactly what Julianna had been thinking that it momentarily stunned her into silence.

"I…I'm certain I don't know," she finally managed.

"I hate to admit it," Mary replied. "But I've never thought about what servants are doing while I'm busy enjoying things like this picnic."

Julianna bit her lip. Once again it was as if her sister had read her mind. "I must admit the same thing."

"They usually tend to disappear after arranging things and return when it's time to take everything away," Mary continued, a guilty look on her face. "Do you think Mr. Worthy and the coachman have anything to eat?"

Julianna sighed. "I'm ashamed to admit it, but I hadn't thought of that before. I…I just assumed they'd eaten before they came. But perhaps they are hungry."

"Should we ask them if they'd like a bun?" Mary asked.

Julianna shook her head. "It seems so improper, but I wouldn't mind sharing." Of course, her own guilt was doubled because here was poor Mary feeling contrite over Mr. Worthy when Julianna happened to know he was a duke who could have a half dozen servants at his beck and call if he only said the word. And stopped playacting.

But now that Mary had brought it up, Julianna couldn't help but wonder if Rhys had brought food for himself. Was he eating it even now on the other side of the coach? She craned her neck but couldn't see what he was doing.

"You're acting quite peculiar today," Mary said, jolting Julianna from her thoughts.

"Pa...pardon?" Julianna replied, guiltily swinging her gaze back to her sister, who was carefully studying her.

Mary set her half-eaten bun on her plate. "Earlier in the carriage you looked as if you might faint, and then you turned red as a cherry, and now you keep glancing back at the coach."

Julianna bit her lip. Oh, lovely, she was acting insane in front of her sister. No wonder Mary was suspicious of her behavior.

Julianna plucked at the neckline of her yellow gown. "I may have felt a bit warm earlier, but—"

"I don't blame you, really," Mary interrupted with a sly look followed by a giggle.

Julianna frowned and blinked. "Blame me for what?"

"For thinking Mr. Worthy is handsome," Mary replied. "He is. Very. I quite agree."

Julianna's heart thundered in her chest. "Mr. Worthy? Handsome?" If her sister had just informed her that King George himself and all fifteen of his children were standing behind her, she couldn't possibly have been more surprised.

"Yes," Mary replied, nodding knowingly. "I couldn't help

but notice you blush when you saw him this morning and again when he opened the door."

Julianna opened her mouth to speak and shut it again. What could she possibly reply? She wanted the earth to open up and swallow her. Perhaps some sort of lake creature could choose this most welcome of times to crawl out of the nearby body of water and consume her.

"I...I don't know what to say." There, that was as honest as she intended to be at the moment.

"You needn't say anything," Mary replied, pulling the bun from her plate again and taking another bite. "And I promise not to say a word to anyone. Least of all Mr. Worthy himself."

Julianna felt herself blushing again. When had her younger sister become so astute? Instead of prolonging this awkward topic, Julianna set about finishing her bun and a handful of grapes while remaining steadfastly silent.

A few minutes later, Rhys reappeared. He stood near the far edge of the blanket and cleared his throat. "Is there anything I might help you with, milady?"

"Yes, Mr. Worthy," Mary said, springing to her feet. "Will you please keep my sister company while I go take a closer look at the flowers across the lake? I'm convinced they're buttercups and I haven't seen buttercups in an age."

Before Rhys had a chance to reply, Mary had lifted her skirts, spun around and took off along the bank toward the far side of the lake.

Julianna raised her hand above her eyes and squinted. She didn't see any buttercups. Was Mary mad? She watched in agonized silence until her sister disappeared behind a small copse of trees on the far side of the small lake.

"Did you tell her?" Rhys's quiet question made Julianna jump. She hadn't expected her sister to orchestrate private time between herself and a groomsman, for heaven's sake.

This entire outing was not turning out the way she'd hoped at all. She'd expected to rile Rhys by making him perform a variety of petty chores designed to make him want to quit pretending to be a servant. Instead, she found him lowering himself onto the blanket across from her, his wrist lying atop his propped-up knee, staring at her as if it was the most normal thing in the world for them to be alone together this way.

Julianna spared a glance toward the opposite side of the lake. She shouldn't allow Mary out of her sight. Mary was her responsibility, after all. But for the life of her she couldn't bring herself to move from her spot. When she spotted Mary's light pink gown just inside the tree line across the lake, she exhaled a sigh and turned back toward Rhys to answer his question.

"Tell her? Tell her what?" she finally managed to choke out.

"Who I am?" he replied, arching a brow.

"Of course not," Julianna replied. "I promised you I wouldn't tell anyone."

Rhys narrowed his eyes. "They why did she leave so suddenly? I'm willing to believe she enjoys flowers, but that was quite a hasty retreat for a jaunt to see a buttercup."

Julianna had to press her lips together to keep from smiling. It had been a hasty retreat indeed. In fact, she hadn't known her sister had it in her to move so quickly. "Yes, well, she seems to think I have a bit of an infatuation with a certain groomsman."

Rhys looked truly surprised. He pointed at himself. "No. Me?"

Julianna inclined her head and smiled. "Yes, she informed me that I blushed earlier in your presence." Even as she said the words, Julianna regretted them.

"Was *that* why you blushed?" he said, a hint of arrogance creeping back into his tone.

"Certainly not," she replied with a conspiratorial smile that belied her words.

Rhys laughed. "Have designs on a groomsman, do you?"

Julianna froze. This would be another opportune time for that lake creature to appear. She mentally counted to five. No luck. "She said she didn't blame me. She thinks you're handsome too."

Rhys's brows shot up. "Too?"

"I mean...*she* thinks you're handsome." This time Julianna was seriously considering jumping into the lake to find the creature herself. Much more expedient and it would keep her from saying more idiotic things.

"I see," Rhys replied. He leaned forward and began putting empty plates back into the basket. "So, I'm to believe your sister is trying to give you time alone with a groomsman?" Skepticism rode his brow.

"It does appear that way," Julianna replied, nodding. "Believe me, if she knew who you truly are, she'd be more likely to stamp on your foot than rush away so we could be alone. She knows how..." She let her sentence die away and swallowed.

He paused and met her gaze. "Stamp on my foot, eh? Why's that?"

Julianna turned her face away. She'd been so close to saying something she never wanted him to know. That Mary knew how upset she'd been when he'd left her that Season.

"She knows the Duke of Worthington is the man who..." She could not bring herself to finish the sentence. It had been too long. The hurt too deep.

"The man who what?" Rhys prompted.

"The man who once courted me," she blurted, hoping her answer would bring an end to this torturous conversation. She needed to change the subject, quickly. "May I ask you something?"

"Of course," he replied, continuing to put the items in the basket. "As long as I may ask you something in return."

Julianna honestly had to consider it for a moment. She did have a question for him, one she wanted him to answer truthfully, but what if his question in return was too difficult for her to answer?

"Very well," she finally replied.

"By all means, you ask first," he offered.

She took a deep breath to steady herself before saying, "It couldn't have been just an idle bet that made you and your friends decide to be servants. What else is the plan?"

He finished loading the basket by putting the empty teapot inside. "What do you mean?"

"I mean there must be some additional reason you're all playacting the way you are. What is it?" She studied his face. He *was* handsome, bless it all, but why did Mary have to point it out?

"Ah, quite astute of you, milady," he replied. He'd drawn up both knees again and his arms rested atop them. "You're right. There is another reason."

"Which is?" she prodded.

He bit his lip and seemed to be struggling with himself as to whether he should tell her. "The truth is, Kendall is looking for a wife."

Julianna's eyes shot open wide and so did her mouth. "By pretending to be a footman?"

"Yes," Rhys replied. "It may sound unconventional, but he has his reasons."

She settled back onto the blanket and managed to close her mouth at least. "I'd say 'unconventional' is an under-statement."

Rhys shrugged. "That's the entire point."

"What is? I don't understand." She frowned.

Rhys leaned back against his wrists. He was casual. That

had been something else she'd liked about him. In their world, they'd been born to be prim and proper. Never a hair out of place, never a bend to the wrist, never a sag to the back. But whenever she and Rhys had been alone together like they were now, he'd acted like a human being, not a fastidious duke. And he didn't seem to mind that she acted normal either. In fact, he'd seemed to like that about her. It was more than she could say for the Marquess of Murdock. No, *Richard*. She needed to get used to thinking of him as Richard. Richard seemed nothing but pleased when she was perfect.

"Kendall wants to see how the young ladies act when they don't know they're in the presence of an earl," Rhys said.

Julianna's mouth fell open once again. "You cannot be serious."

Rhys leaned back farther and narrowed his eyes on her. "I'm quite serious. That is a hazard of having a title, you know?"

She frowned at him. "What is?"

His jaw tightened. "Young women pretending they're interested in you when they're really only interested in your title." His words carried an unmistakable trace of anger.

She dropped her gaze to the pattern of the quilt and traced a fingertip around it. "Lady Emily Foswell," she said in almost a whisper. The entire *ton* knew that Lady Emily had tossed over the future Earl of Kendall days before their wedding when an offer from a baron came along.

"Precisely," Rhys replied, his jaw still tight.

Julianna decided to move the conversation away from things like offers and titles. The look on his face and the anger in his tone made her uncomfortable. She couldn't risk getting into an argument with him with Mary no doubt on her way back. "I still don't understand why you all thought no one would recognize you here."

"Is it so outlandish?" Rhys replied. "Think about it. How many people in the dining room recognize Kendall each night when he's serving them?"

Julianna pursed her lips and nodded. She knew precisely what he meant. She had thought about it. She'd been astounded, actually, when her own mother had not noticed the Earl of Kendall serving dinner in the dining room. Julianna had watched Kendall surreptitiously for the last two nights and decided the man did an excellent job of pretending to be a servant. But no one seemed to look at him long enough or give him enough attention to realize a peer of the realm was serving them roast duck.

"I find it sad, actually, how easily Lord Kendall has been able to stride about the dining room filling water glasses without anyone noticing him." She sighed. "It says something awful about our Society, doesn't it?"

"It does," Rhys replied. His voice was pensive as well.

"I admit, I didn't notice myself until halfway through the first meal, which means I'm nearly as bad as everyone else." She shook her head.

"You're in excellent company," Rhys replied. "There is more than one peer in that room from what I've been told. None of them have noticed either."

She plucked at the blanket. "I still don't think it's a good idea for Lord Kendall to try to find a wife in that manner."

Rhys cocked his head to the side. "I'll be certain to tell Kendall to steer clear of *you*, then." He took a breath, all trace of humor gone. "Oh, but you're already betrothed, aren't you?"

CHAPTER ELEVEN

Rhys spurred Alabaster over the next hilltop. He'd been riding hell-for-leather across the hilly terrain that comprised Clayton's property for the better part of the last hour. It was time to let the fine horse take a break.

Rhys hadn't been able to ride fast enough. He hadn't been able to ride far enough to rid his thoughts of his unsatisfying conversation with Julianna at the lake this morning.

He'd mentioned her being betrothed and before Julianna had had a chance to reply, Mary had returned with her arms full of buttercups, and he'd had to go back to pretending to be a dutiful servant. He'd gathered the basket and the blanket and escorted the two young women back to the coach. Then he'd ridden behind on the running board while a thousand thoughts had raced through his mind. The same thoughts that were plaguing him now.

She knows the Duke of Worthington is the man who... Julianna had let that sentence trail off and when he'd pressed her on it, she'd said, *is the man who once courted me.* But Rhys knew. He *knew* she'd meant to say something else. Something that indicated she blamed him for their falling out. He'd long suspected she blamed him. But today he'd been certain of it.

She'd shook away the topic so casually, so quickly, as if she honestly believed she'd been in the right about the entire situation. Sometimes she seemed caring and thoughtful, like when she'd mentioned how sad a commentary on Society it was that none of the other guests had recognized Kendall in the dining room. But she was the same woman who'd pretended to be falling in love with him in order to marry the bachelor with the most esteemed title.

He refused to think about how she'd said she found him attractive. That did nothing but confuse matters. What she meant to say was she found his wealth and title attractive. She knew precisely who he really was.

He continued to walk Alabaster for several more minutes before rubbing him down with a towel from the saddlebag and tying him to the fence. This was the same stop he'd come to the first day here with Julianna. Damn it. Why did everything remind him of her? She hadn't been in his thoughts for years. Well, months. Very well, perhaps weeks. But *that* was only because he'd seen her father at the tailor's in London recently.

The man had barely acknowledged him. Montlake detested him. Not because Rhys had courted his daughter and failed to offer for her. Well, not *only* for that reason. No, Montlake was the type who scorned gambling and drinking, and well, those were Rhys's two favorite pastimes. Montlake hated him for his wicked ways. No doubt he'd been nothing but pleased that Rhys's courtship of his daughter had ended in naught.

That made two of them.

Rhys had just finished wrapping Alabaster's leather reins around the fence post when the thunder of hooves behind him made him turn. Raising his hand above his eyes, he squinted across the sun-filled meadow. A single rider leaning low upon a horse, was headed directly toward him.

Soon Julianna's form came into view. She was leaning forward and swiping at Violet's hindquarters with her crop. Dust flew beneath the horse's hooves and moments later, Rhys realized that she was riding...astride.

He waited, hands on hips, until Violet slowed to a stop in front of him as Julianna sat up, tugged at the reins, and called, "Whoa."

"There you are," she said next, smiling at him as if they hadn't had an awkward exchange the last time they'd seen each other.

"You ride astride now?" he asked, sarcasm dripping from his voice.

"I've ridden astride forever," she replied jauntily, "I simply used to care what you thought of me and now I don't."

Despite himself, he respected her for that pert answer. "I was looking to be alone for a bit," he ground out. "I'm certain one of the other groomsmen can help you this afternoon."

"Not with this," she replied, swinging one breeches-clad leg over the saddle and nimbly jumping to the ground. She landed on her booted feet and looked up at him. "I want to ask you something, Rhys."

Both the urgency in her voice and the sight of her in the leg-hugging breeches made his pulse quicken. He didn't *want* to want to hear what she had to say, but he admitted to himself that he did. As for the breeches, he tried not to look.

Tried and failed because when she turned from him to tie Violet's reins to the nearby fence post near Alabaster, Julianna's backside was presented to him in its skin-tight kid leather, and he clenched his jaw. In addition to her breeches, she wore a white shirt buttoned up the front, with a wide gap at the throat that revealed her creamy skin and *décolletage*. Surely her mother didn't know she was out riding astride on

Clayton's property. Had the other groomsmen seen her like this? They must have. He wanted to punch the other groomsmen.

"What do you want to ask me?" he said, clearing his throat.

As soon as Violet was secure, Julianna swiveled to face him, while he pretended as if his gaze had not just whipped up to her face the moment she'd turned.

"You know about my engagement?" she began, a bit breathlessly.

Ah, so that was it. She hadn't liked their earlier discussion ending on that note any more than he had. "Doesn't the entire *ton* know about it?" he ground out.

She took a deep breath. "Perhaps, but I specifically wondered if *you* did. I know the announcement was in the paper, but I couldn't help but wonder if you had seen it or been told."

He cleared his throat again and mimicked an overly proper voice. "Lady Julianna Montgomery, fresh from her failure with the Duke of Worthington, seems to have set her sights on the *next* most eligible bachelor in London, the Marquess of Murdock." His eyes bore into her. "Wasn't that what the *Times* wrote?"

Julianna swallowed and leaned back, closing her eyes. "You were…hurt by it?"

"Ha," he scoffed.

She clenched her jaw. "I suppose it's *my* fault, for not waiting around for a man who lied when he said he would return soon."

Rhys's nostrils flared. How dare she try to blame him. "And I suppose when one man is no longer available, any man will do for *the most popular debutante of the Season*."

She tossed a hand in the air. "That was nothing more than gossip."

He arched a brow. "What was?"

"Everything they printed in the *Times*."

He crossed his arms over his chest. "Really? Seemed entirely believable to me."

"The *Times* writes whatever will sell the most newspapers. You know that, Rhys. I've seen more than one story detailing your drunken nights at the gambling hells. Are you telling me those were all true?"

He scratched the back of his neck. So, she kept up with him through the paper, did she? Perhaps that's how she'd known how eligible a bachelor he was. "Unfortunately, most of them probably were," he admitted.

Still holding her riding crop, she put her hands on her hips. "You're telling me that you've *never* been the target of the gossip columns' maliciousness?"

He expelled his breath and tried not to notice how good her hips looked in those breeches. Her hips, her legs, and her — He forced himself to concentrate on what she'd just said.

"I suppose I have, a time or two," he replied. Or two dozen. The rags were always pairing him off with some scandalous woman as his latest mistress or reporting that he'd lost far more money than he actually had. He bowed his head and kicked at the dirt with his boot. "Are you telling me you're not really engaged to Murdock?"

Damn. Why was there a part of him that hoped she would answer 'yes,' even as he knew she wouldn't?

"No," she replied. "That part is true. But the part about me 'setting my sights on the next most eligible bachelor in London' was completely false. At least, that's not at all how I recall it happening."

"Ah, a shoddy memory," he said, scorn audible in his voice. "Happens to the best of us, doesn't it?" He lifted his head to face her again. "Perhaps that's why I never came back. I forgot."

"You left!" Her voice rose and color streamed into her cheeks. "You gave no explanation for it. That article in the *Times* didn't come out until *after* you'd been gone for well over nine months. Nine months in which you wrote to me once and told me that you—let me see, how did you put it— you 'hoped I hadn't thought more of our *acquaintance* than you had.'"

"I just told you. It slipped my mind," he ground out.

"You're lying," she shot back. "What was it? What was the *real* reason you left, Rhys? You owe me that much." Julianna's eyes flashed and she'd tossed back her head. She looked magnificent, standing up against him, the wind whipping her hair in gold silken strands across her face.

"I did you a favor," Rhys spit out. The words were bitter on his tongue, but they were true.

"Oh, leaving me? Humiliating me? Those are *favors* as far as you're concerned?"

Rhys bit the inside of his cheek hard. Had he been wrong all these months? Or was she playacting still, just telling him the thing he wanted to hear? Damn it. He may have given her her freedom, but he'd found out later how close he'd come to being trapped by her acting. Was she acting now too? She had to be. She hadn't written back and asked questions. No, she'd moved on. "You certainly didn't waste time finding someone to replace me. The 'next most eligible bachelor,' to be precise."

Her eyes flashed green fire. She stepped up to him. "Oh, and you're not hurt? You liar."

"You would know. Takes a liar to know one." He smiled at her smugly.

"What did I ever lie about?" she flung back at him.

He took a step closer to her; staring into her eyes, they were barely a pace away from each other. He leaned down until their lips were merely an inch apart. A muscle ticked in his jaw. "Tell me, Julianna, was it difficult pretending to want me?"

Her head snapped to the side as if he'd slapped her, and her nostrils flared. He knew his words had been crass, but he had to know for sure, had to see the truth in her eyes, had to know once and for all if it had been an act.

When she slowly turned her face back to him, her eyes still smoldered with anger, but he saw something else too, and he recognized it as the truth. "No," she said, her voice low and sultry, her gaze holding his. "Unfortunately, it's *never* been difficult to want you, Rhys."

"Damn you," he breathed.

"Damn you," she echoed, the words coming out through clenched teeth. Her breasts were heaving, her chest rising and falling with each heavy breath.

"You're a liar," he accused.

"No, *you* are," she retorted.

With a growl of surrender, Rhys's arms snaked out and he pulled her savagely to him. Crushing her body against his, he held her tight, his mouth swooping down to claim hers.

The moment their lips met, his tongue forced her lips apart and he kissed her with all the pent-up longing and passion he'd felt for her every day since he'd met her, every day since he'd left her. He had to know if it was as good as he remembered.

Part of his brain waited for her to push him away, but she didn't. Instead, her arms wrapped around his neck and she pulled him down even closer. He pushed her against the fence post that came up to the middle of her back and he ground his hips against hers. She kissed him mindlessly, as if they'd never kissed before, as if it were the first time, as if they'd never fought, never left each other.

Her hands wrapped themselves through his hair and she clung to his neck and matched him thrust for thrust with her tongue. His hands were on his hips, pulling her toward him, then reaching down her backside. He yanked her tight against his rock-hard erection. The outline of her firm arse through the breeches drove him mad. He could touch her this way forever and never get his fill.

And then they were tumbling to the grass, fumbling with each other's clothing. They rolled together until they were on the far side of the fence behind the tree line, where they couldn't be seen from the stables. He ripped open her shirt with both hands and freed her breasts to his grasp in a matter of moments. His mouth traveled a hot trail down her face, chin, and throat until he sucked her nipple into his mouth.

Julianna cried out, cradling his head in her hands. "Rhys," she called. "Rhys."

His lips moved back up to her neck where he sucked and kissed her. Meanwhile, her lips were at his ear, panting, her small tongue darting inside, making his body buck.

Her hand reached down to rub the outline of his cock beneath his breeches. He clenched his jaw and moaned. Then his mouth descended to her breasts again and he lavished each one thoroughly with his tongue and lips, sucking gently, then hard, tugging at them with his teeth until she called his name again.

She squeezed him through his breeches and Rhys wanted to come like an untried lad. Instead, he twisted his hips away and minutes later, he forced himself to pull his mouth away from her gorgeous breasts. He meant to only stop momentarily, to see if she was all right, to catch his breath for one timeless moment. He pressed his forehead hard against hers, his breath coming out in hard, short, pants.

She was breathing heavily too, her chest still rising and falling beneath the tatters of her shirt. He was beyond jealous of that shirt at the moment. "Rhys," she breathed again. "Rhys."

He knew this shouldn't continue, but he couldn't help himself. He leaned down and kissed her lips once more.

She pressed a hand to his chest, pushing him back.

He stopped, staring at her. His harsh breath hurt his lungs.

"We must stop, Rhys," she whispered.

He pressed his forehead to hers once more. "Why?" he whispered. "Tell me, why?"

"Because," her voice was pained but resolute, "I'm betrothed to the Marquess of Murdock."

The lust in his eyes quickly faded. "You remembered that, did you?"

CHAPTER TWELVE

Julianna stole to her bedchamber window that night. She pushed the curtains aside as was her wont and stared up at the glowing full moon. She wrapped her arms around herself tight and for the first time since that afternoon, allowed herself to think about what had happened.

She had kissed Rhys. With enthusiasm. She could hardly pretend it hadn't been mutual. Oh, God. Where had all her outrage gone? Where had the anger at the months of heartache he'd put her through flown the moment his lips touched hers? The man was detestable. She'd kissed Detestable, of all people!

The worst part was…she'd enjoyed it.

He'd denied having been hurt by her engagement announcement in the paper but, dear God, he had quoted it word-for-humiliating-word. She'd never dreamed he read the gossip pages of the *Times*. She supposed it had been *naïve* of her to assume he'd never heard about her engagement or that someone hadn't brought it to his attention, but…she'd *never* imagined he'd been hurt by it. He was the one who left and never returned, after all. However, the fact remained that he'd sounded angry when he'd repeated the printed words. *Was* he hurt? How was that possible?

Well, she'd been hurt too. That's why she'd fired back with that bit about him lying about returning that Season. Only then he'd said, *I suppose when one man is no longer available, any man will do for the most popular debutante of the Season.* That had hurt too. Is that what he thought about her? Truly? Is that what he'd believed all these months? That she'd quickly tossed him over for the next eligible bachelor?

It still didn't explain why he'd left. Her engagement announcement hadn't come out in the paper until well into her third Season. He might have been angry about it, but that certainly wasn't what had caused him to leave and not return. No. Rhys was being disingenuous. Doing his best to appear the injured party when they both knew *precisely* what had happened between them.

The kiss had been entirely unexpected. Perhaps wrong, but necessary as far as Julianna was concerned. Or at least that's what she'd told herself earlier tonight as she'd tossed and turned in her bed. The kiss had been necessary, she reasoned, because it told her more clearly and powerfully than any words could that Rhys had not stopped having feelings for her.

All this time, these many months, she'd been dogged by the notion that he'd left her because he'd only been play-acting with her to begin with. That he'd never truly felt anything for her. But she knew now beyond any doubt that not only had he felt something, he still felt it. Or at least could if circumstances were different.

She also realized that Rhys had a secret. He'd hinted at it, at least, when he'd said he'd 'done her a favor' by leaving her that spring. What did he mean? His reply had been vague. But she'd long suspected he'd left for something more than a visit to the country to see his mother. He'd been gone too long. Had written too little.

She'd eventually decided it had just been his way of disengaging from her, but now she suspected more than ever that there had been another reason for his defection. Whatever it was, he didn't seem inclined to share it with her. Not that it mattered now. One kiss couldn't change the months of pain they'd put each other through. One kiss didn't change the fact that she was engaged to the Marquess of Murdock.

And Rhys still didn't trust her. That much was obvious. They'd kissed each other passionately, but she'd seen the disgust in his eyes when she'd reminded him that she was engaged. And she could feel the judgement in his tone. She knew it. He thought she had pretended to want him because of his title. The thought made her want to scream. Was he such a fool that he couldn't see how much she truly wanted him? Had always wanted him? She shook her head. That was the trouble. She'd *wanted* that horse's arse.

"Anna?" Mary's soft voice called from behind her.

Julianna turned, letting the curtain drop closed again and sealing the room in darkness. "I'm sorry, Mary. Did I wake you?"

The flame of a single candle sprang to life on Mary's bedside table, then Mary stood, carrying the candle to the window.

"What are you doing awake at this hour?" Mary asked when she reached Julianna's side.

Julianna sighed. "I couldn't sleep."

"Is it because of Mr. Worthy?" Mary's sleepy voice asked next.

"What? Why would you ask that?" Julianna's heart began to pound painfully in her chest.

"I don't know," Mary replied, setting the candle upon the

windowsill. "It just seemed to me that...never mind, I'm sorry to have mentioned it. Forgive me."

Forgive her? The poor dear. Mary was more astute than Julianna or their parents ever gave her credit for. She might be the quiet one, the cautious one, but Mary was always watching and paying attention and thinking about other people's feelings.

"No, Mary, it's I who should apologize. You're right." Julianna hung her head "It actually does have something to do with Mr. Worthy."

Mary's brow furrowed. "You don't have to tell me if you don't want to, Anna. But I'm here if you do want to talk about it."

Julianna reached out and hugged her sister. "Oh, Mary, you're such a dear."

"I promise not to repeat anything you say."

"Of course, you wouldn't." Julianna trusted her sister with her life. But there was a secret she'd promised not to tell also, and she took her promise quite seriously, too. She could tell Mary that she'd kissed the groomsman, Mr. Worthy, but she was still not at liberty to reveal Rhys's true identity.

Julianna turned and rested her shoulder against the window frame. "The truth is...I kissed Mr. Worthy today."

Mary sucked in her breath, then tentatively leaned forward to watch Julianna's face. She retrieved the candle and held it higher. "Truly?"

Julianna swallowed and nodded. "Yes. I...I don't know why. I couldn't help myself."

"At the lake?" Mary asked.

"No, not at the lake. Later...in the meadow."

A small smile popped to Mary's lips. "I think I know why you did it, Anna," she said. "He's ever so handsome." A frown quickly replaced Mary's smile. "But Lord Murdock..."

Julianna paced away from her sister, wrapping her arms

tightly around her middle. "I know. I know. I've no excuse. I feel terrible. I wish I could go back in time and erase it from having ever happened."

"Oh, Anna. Don't judge yourself too harshly." Her sister came up behind her and placed a warm hand on her shoulder. "You're only human. Like the vicar says, we all make mistakes."

Julianna patted her sister's hand. Mary would never make a mistake like that and they both knew it. Julianna was the impetuous one. But Mary was so kind and forgiving that she would never judge another soul for making a mistake. Even one as large as this one. "Thank you, Mary, but I know it was wrong. It never should have happened."

"Does Mr. Worthy know that you're engaged to be married?" Mary asked quietly.

Julianna bit her lip. The truth would paint them both in a worse light, but there was no sense not telling it. She'd already admitted to the worst part. "Yes. He knows," she said softly, lowering her chin to her chest.

Pulling her hand from Julianna's shoulder, Mary moved in front of her to face her again. "Oh, Anna, anyone can make a mistake. You're not actually married yet. That's what truly matters. And of course, you won't do something like that again."

Julianna swallowed. She wanted to say of course not, but instead all she could muster was a half-hearted nod. "Thank you for not hating me."

Mary gave her another hug. She squeezed her tight. "Oh, Anna, you're my sister. I love you. I'd never hate you, no matter what you did."

"Thank you, Mary."

"It's all right," Mary said, nodding. "I hope you're able to get some rest, Anna." Mary took the candle and crawled back into bed.

Julianna forced herself to return to her bed as well. She pulled the blankets to her chin and stared up at the dark ceiling. She already knew she would return to the stables on some other pretense tomorrow, just as she knew she had no business doing so and that she would eventually regret it. But she couldn't help herself. She couldn't let it be. Rhys thought she was after him for his title? No. She was still after him for revenge. At least that's what she told herself. She was beginning to have her doubts.

"Anna," came Mary's soft voice a few minutes later. "Whatever you're thinking, I just want to say that I don't think you should marry someone whom you don't love, no matter what Mama and Papa say."

CHAPTER THIRTEEN

Rhys had long ago given up trying to get comfortable on the hay-filled mattress. He'd abandoned it and walked to the end of the long loft above the stables where he stared out at the silver-white full moon.

He might be a drinker and a gambler and generally interested in his own amusements, but it had been a long time since he'd lost control the way he had this afternoon with Julianna.

He pounded his fist against the wooden beam above his head. Damn it. He had absolutely no excuse for what he'd done today, kissing Julianna, touching her. He'd been the veriest rogue.

And she may have stopped their kiss this afternoon, but she certainly had been a willing participant for several minutes before that. Rhys had to wonder if she would be willing to toss Murdock aside if Rhys asked her to. His stomach clenched.

And even if she truly loved him and always had, after what his good friend Kendall had been through, Rhys knew he could never marry a lady who was betrothed to another man. It was wrong. Plain and simple.

And Julianna Montgomery was most definitely engaged.

It was so official it had been in the paper.

If she left Murdock for him, she'd essentially be doing what Lady Emily did, and that was unacceptable. Rhys could never live with that and neither should Julianna.

If she had been acting this afternoon, she'd been convincing, he had to admit. The lust between them had not been faked. He knew that now. He'd seen the truth in her eyes just before he kissed her.

Leaving me? Humiliating me? Those are favors as far as you're concerned? she'd said. His skin had gone hot then cold when she'd said that. He'd never considered the timing of all it of before. At least, he'd never considered how it all must have seemed to *her*. He had been gone for nine months. He'd been so preoccupied with his reason for leaving town and the secrecy surrounding it, he hadn't thought much about the fact that the entire time she'd been expecting an offer. It made sense that she would have been hurt by his leaving. It made sense that she would have been humiliated even. Guilt tugged at him.

But he mustn't forget about the blasted story in the paper. When it had come out, he'd been incensed. Influenced by Kendall's past with Lady Emily, Rhys had been convinced that Julianna had only been playacting at wanting him because of his title.

Christ, had Julianna been hurt too, or was she acting now also? He didn't know anything for certain. He only knew she'd been right about one thing. He *had* been hurt. The story in the paper about her choosing the next most eligible bachelor had wounded him far more than he ever wanted to admit.

And he'd been right about something too. He had, in fact, done her a favor by not returning.

CHAPTER FOURTEEN

The debutantes marched two-by-two through the doors to the stables the next morning. There was a total of six of them, led by Julianna and her sister. They were dressed in a variety of pastel-colored gowns with matching parasols and gloves and delicate slippers.

Rhys watched them file in with a wry smile on his face. It looked like bloody Almack's in here today. He could only guess at what new torment Julianna intended to subject him to. No doubt spurred on by his rude comment after their kiss yesterday about her remembering she was betrothed to Murdock. Excellent.

"What's this, ye reckon'?" Mr. Hereford asked, pushing back his hat with his thumb and rubbing his forehead as he watched the giggling group of ladies fluttered into the middle of the stables, pointing and exclaiming at nearly everything they saw.

"If I don't mistake my guess," Rhys drawled, "they've come to make my life not worth living today."

Mr. Hereford gave Rhys a sympathetic glance before

jogging out to greet Julianna. "Good mornin', me lady," he said, bowing to her. "'ow may we 'elp ye, this fine morn'?"

Rhys turned his back and continued mucking out the stall in which he was standing.

"Good morning, Mr. Hereford," Julianna replied in her most obliging tone. "So good to see you again. I was hoping my friends and I might go on a ride around the grounds today. Do you have a coach big enough for all of us?"

"Indeed, we do, Lady Julianna. Lord Clayton keeps his break here at the estate. Today would be a lovely day for a ride in it."

The open-topped, four-wheeled carriage was a popular conveyance in the country. Often used for hunting expeditions, it was similarly perfect for six ladies to travel about and see the estate grounds.

"Oh, the break will be perfect," Julianna replied. "I do hope you have a couple of groomsmen who might accompany us. I was thinking Mr. Worthy would do."

Rhys sighed and straightened. There it was. Her entire reason for coming here today, dressed up in some pretty speech and a seemingly off-handed remark that he might accompany them.

He propped his pitchfork against the stall door and dusted off his hands on his breeches. He would have to change out of his muck-ridden clothing before he could accompany the ladies. He might as well get to it.

Mr. Hereford had already turned around to look for him. The older man knew Rhys would have to prepare himself. Rhys pointed up to indicate he'd go get dressed before disappearing up the staircase to the loft.

Once upstairs, Rhys quickly stripped off his dirty clothes, wiped himself down with soap and water from the wash bowl, and hastily threw on his livery before dashing his fingers through his hair and racing back downstairs.

Mr. Hereford hadn't been idle. He and two of the other groomsmen had put the horses to the break and the conveyance was waiting in the center of the stables by the time Rhys returned.

"There he is," Mr. Hereford said, his smile widening as soon as he saw Rhys. No doubt the older man was eager to get the ladies out of the stables and on their way. Their chatter had increased, and Mr. Hereford looked at a loss for what else to say to them.

Rhys strode forward and bowed to the ladies.

"Good morning, Mr. Worthy," Julianna said with a prim smile. "I was hoping you wouldn't mind taking me and my friends on a jaunt around the grounds today."

Rhys executed his most perfect bow. "It would be my pleasure, my lady."

The other ladies were sent into a fit of giggles.

Rhys glanced at each of the young women. Besides Julianna and Mary, he'd never met any of the other four. No doubt Julianna had picked them carefully to ensure they wouldn't know who he was. How kind of her. "Henry and I would be honored to accompany you," he continued.

Henry, one of the other groomsmen, bowed as well. "At your service, Lady Julianna."

Rhys gave Henry a reassuring nod. Henry was the best choice to join them. He was smart and discreet. He knew who Rhys really was, but he stood the best chance at keeping up the pretense for an entire morning without any breaks in his performance. Good chap, Henry.

After Rhys and Henry helped all six of the ladies up into the break and had duly asked if any of them needed their legs warmed by a blanket, Ernest took his seat on the raised box while Rhys and Henry stood on small platforms at the rear on opposite sides of the wheels.

Julianna, he noted, had taken a seat in the middle, facing

the back on the same side he was standing. She was no more than a few feet away from him and her haughty smile indicated she intended to make this entire outing as difficult for him as possible. Perfect. Apparently, she was still bent on revenge.

The carriage soon took off out of the stables and into the bright morning sunlight. The smell of newly cut grass and blooming flowers wafted along the slight breeze. The top was down so the ladies could see all around them. Their bonneted heads swiveled to look at everything. Their chatter did not abate until they came to their first stop, the flower gardens behind the library.

"Do tell us what we're looking at, Mr. Worthy," Julianna called, her gloved hand atop her hat. "Being *employed* here, I assume you're quite familiar with the grounds of Clayton Manor."

"Of course," he replied, his most obliging smile pinned to his face. "These are his lordship's flower gardens. I believe his mother had them installed and personally sees to their care when she visits."

"Where is his lordship's mother?" Julianna asked next. "Does she live nearby?"

"She has a town house in London, my lady, but when she is in the country, she lives at the Dower house near the front of the estate. I believe we'll be passing by it later. I'll be certain to point it out."

She was obviously trying to trip him up. But Rhys had known Clayton since they were barely more than lads. He knew enough about the estate to give an informal tour, for Christ's sake, and what he didn't know he fully intended to invent. He refused to allow Julianna to ruffle him.

"Does she come to visit Lord Clayton often, Mr. Worthy?" Julianna asked next.

"I wouldn't know," Rhys replied without missing a beat. "I

am a stable servant, my lady. I'm not often in the house, save for occasional meals, and Lord Clayton prefers his servants not to gossip." He gave Julianna a complacent smile and arched a brow at her as if to say, *There. Find fault with that.*

She pressed her lips together and gave him a look that said, *Well-played.*

Next, the conveyance rattled on past the meadow and out to the lake. The same place they'd been for their picnic with Mary. When the break came to a stop, the ladies' chatter ceased once again and they all looked expectantly at Rhys, anticipating that Julianna would ask him more questions.

"How many fish are stocked in the lake, Mr. Worthy?" Julianna dutifully asked.

"As I am not the groundskeeper, my lady, I'm not entirely certain, but I do know his lordship has caught both pike and perch here in abundance. I have also heard that my lord and lady have planned a picnic for the guests here tomorrow."

The ladies must have liked that response because their chatter increased, and a general air of excitement was in their tone.

"Oh, please, Anna, can't we take a quick walk along the shoreline?" Mary begged.

Julianna looked at Rhys. "Mr. Worthy? Would we be able to take a walk along the water? Is there time?"

"Whatever you wish, my lady," he replied agreeably.

The ladies conferred for a few moments before deciding it *would* be lovely to take a stroll by the lake. Rhys and Henry hopped down from their spots and helped all six women to alight.

Mary and three of the ladies all took off at a decent clip to look for the buttercups she'd promised them. Julianna and one other young woman walked more slowly toward the edge of the water nearby. Rhys strode along behind them to continue answering questions.

"Mr. Worthy," Julianna soon asked, "what is the depth of the lake?"

Rhys did not hesitate. "It's approximately fifteen and a quarter meters, my lady."

She turned and gave him a look that clearly indicated she knew he'd made that up.

He returned it with a look that clearly indicated he knew she could never prove it.

She paused for a moment at the water's edge and thoughtfully tapped her cheek with one gloved finger. "Mr. *Worthy?* An interesting name is it not, Helen?" she said to her companion. Julianna then turned to Rhys. "You don't happen to be any relation to the Duke of Worthington, do you?"

Helen was staring at the water and as a result, was unable to see Rhys blink his eyes slowly at Julianna while wearing a false smile and giving her an *I'm-going-to-make-you-pay-for-this* look. "Not to my knowledge, my lady, but I certainly wouldn't mind discovering I'm a relation. I hear the current duke is handsome, wealthy, and charming."

Helen took the opportunity to speak. "I have also heard he's handsome, but he may not be wealthy. According to my Papa, he gambles a great deal and has lost his fortune. Though he's still quite eligible, of that there can be no doubt."

"Well, I can assure you rumors of his charm have been *greatly* exaggerated," Julianna added with a tight smile.

Helen giggled at that.

"I doubt that," Rhys replied, his tone clipped. "He's visited Clayton Manor upon occasion. I've met him. I found him to be *quite* charming. Witty, too."

"He certainly *thinks* he's witty," Julianna replied.

More giggling from Helen.

They went on that way for several more minutes before the other ladies returned each carrying a plucked buttercup in their hands.

"The flowers are beautiful on the far side of the lake," one of them exclaimed.

"Yes, well, we may want to return to the carriage, my lady," Rhys said to Julianna. "We still have a great deal more to see if you would like the entire tour."

"Indeed," Julianna replied as she began ushering her friends back toward the carriage.

As they walked, one of the ladies said, "I've been having the loveliest time at the party so far, but I cannot help but be disappointed that more of Lord Clayton's friends aren't in attendance."

"Like whom?" Julianna asked, clearly relishing the topic. She gave Rhys a sideways glance.

"The Earl of Kendall should be here," one of the other ladies said.

"Yes, and the Marquess of Bellingham," another added.

"Perhaps even the Duke of Worthington," a third pointed out.

They'd arrived back at the break and Henry caught Rhys's gaze and arched a brow. Rhys slightly shook his head.

"I've heard none of them can countenance *ton* events," Lady Helen said, regret in her tone. "Which is terribly disappointing, because that's the only reason Mama brought me here."

"Yes, well, let's not talk about the Duke of Worthington," Mary pointed out loyally, glancing apprehensively at Julianna.

"Oh, that's right, Mary," the first lady said. "We don't want to talk about that blackguard. Not in front of our dear Julianna, here, do we?"

Julianna shrugged. She didn't meet Rhys's gaze. "It's quite all right, Lady Agnes. I've all but forgotten about the Duke of Worthington."

"Just as well," Lady Agnes replied. "He's known to be a drunken lout. You're much better off without him."

"Don't I know it?" Julianna replied, a beatific smile on her face. She still wouldn't look at him, the coward.

Henry shot him another quick glance, which Rhys did not return.

"It's the funniest thing, but we were just speaking of him," Lady Helen added.

"Of Worthington?" Mary asked, her brow furrowed.

"Yes," Lady Helen replied. "I've heard something about him being in debt."

"I heard that too," Lady Agnes replied.

"According to the *Times*, he's lost far more than he's ever won at the gaming tables," the third lady reported.

"I hear he likes to make outrageous bets with his friends as well," Julianna added.

This time Rhys glowered at Julianna. None of the other ladies were looking at him, thank God.

Moments later, they all piled back into the coach, Julianna looking like the cat who swallowed the canary, and they were soon off toward the far end of the grounds.

The next stop on their tour was a trip out to the far edge of the property where the forested grounds hid the small gamekeeper's cottage.

"Is the gamekeeper at home?" Julianna wanted to know.

"I don't believe so, my lady—he usually arrives in September just before hunting season begins. But I'm happy to go knock at his door if you'd like to make certain."

"No, thank you, Mr. Worthy," Julianna replied. "I wouldn't want you to get shot." She blinked at him, her tone implying the opposite.

To finish off the tour, they cut across the far meadow back to the front of the property to meet the meticulously maintained grand drive up to the manor house. Then, they wound down the small lane to the Dower House. The entire way, Julianna peppered Rhys with a variety of questions about the estate's architecture, landscaping, number of servants, and any other random bit of information she could think of. She was obviously enjoying herself. Especially when the women had all spoken ill of Rhys. No doubt that had been her favorite part of the outing.

By the time they returned to the stables, it was past noon and all the ladies looked a bit tired. All of them except Julianna. *She* looked as if she were fit to keep touring the grounds and asking him endless rounds of questions all day. No doubt she'd enjoy it.

As Rhys and Henry assisted the ladies out of the carriage, Rhys ensured he helped Julianna down himself. She was the last to disembark. The other ladies had all walked ahead toward the entrance of the stables, no doubt eager to return to the manor house for luncheon and rest.

Rhys stopped Julianna momentarily with a hand to her forearm. "You're *trying* to rile me, aren't you?"

She folded her hands together primly, swinging her parasol between them. "Riling you is no more than the embroidery upon the handkerchief. I'm hoping to get you to quit and forfeit your bet."

"It won't work," he declared adamantly.

"We'll see," she replied sweetly.

CHAPTER FIFTEEN

Julianna had clearly chosen poorly this morning, she thought to herself later that afternoon as she took a solitary stroll through the gardens. Rhys loved to talk. Asking him to take the ladies on a tour of the grounds this morning had not been a particularly taxing chore for him. He'd somehow managed to answer every question she'd concocted and some of them she'd made up at the last moment.

Julianna had, however, chosen the ladies carefully. She'd picked each one based on the fact that they'd only been in Society for one Season and didn't have any older siblings who may have known Worthington.

Of course, she'd experienced a bit of trepidation when they'd first arrived at the stables. No matter how carefully she'd chosen, there was always the chance that one of them happened to know what Rhys looked like. But she'd kept her confident smile in place and so had Rhys, and the afternoon had been not entirely unpleasant. Lord Clayton's estate was lovely, and attempting to trip up Rhys had been nothing if not enjoyable—even if he hadn't exactly risen to the bait.

The best part, however, had definitely been when the ladies began discussing the Duke of Worthington right in front of him. Why, it couldn't have gone better if she'd planned it herself. It had taken every ounce of control she'd had not to look at him.

The part about him being in debt was interesting. She'd heard the odd rumor or two, but she'd never given them much credence. He certainly lived as if he were wealthy. But that didn't mean it wasn't true. Many peers lived on copious amounts of credit. Could Rhys's debts be the reason he was so eager to win the bet? If that was the case, her trying to get him to lose it wouldn't just be a matter of revenge, it might very well break him. Based on the amount of money he'd tried to promise her for her silence, the bet had to be for a large sum of money indeed.

For the first time since this entire game had begun four days ago, Julianna felt the slightest bit of guilt tug at her. What if she caused him to lose and that plunged him into debt from which he could not rebound? She would single-handedly be responsible for the downfall of the Duke of Worthington.

She bit her lip. A few days ago, she would have said that was precisely what she wanted. But now she had her doubts. If she was no longer trying to rile him, however, what possible excuse did she have for going out to the stables to see him each day?

CHAPTER SIXTEEN

The next excuse presented itself to Julianna the following morning, quite conveniently in the person of her younger sister. She and Mary were eating breakfast off of trays that had been brought up to their bedchamber when she turned to her sister and asked, "What would you like to do today?"

Mary finished chewing her orange slice before replying, "I thought we'd go on the picnic planned for lunchtime with the other ladies. But, perhaps this morning..." Her voice trailed off and she bit her lip.

"Yes?" Julianna prodded, taking a bite from her own small bowl of fruit.

Mary's cheeks turned ever-so-slightly pink. "At dinner last night one of the gentlemen asked me if I would care to go riding with him sometime."

Julianna's eyes widened and a catlike smile appeared on her face. "Ooh, which gentleman was it?"

"Lord Mixton," Mary replied, her cheeks turning even more pink.

"Mixton?" Julianna set down her spoon. "He seems nice enough."

"I agree," Mary replied, "and for the first time, I actually wanted to go."

Julianna gave her sister a sympathetic look. "Oh, you poor darling, I know you're scared witless of horses. Perhaps you can ask him to go for a walk instead."

Mary shook her head. "No. No. You misunderstand. My fear of horses is perfectly silly. I know that. It's also quite embarrassing. I would do anything to be like everyone else. To *not* be frightened witless of horses."

Julianna reached over and squeezed her sister's cold hand. "Mary, dear, I don't understand. What are you saying?"

Her sister swallowed hard. "I'm saying I want to make my courage bigger than my fear, Anna. I want to learn to ride a horse."

"Learn to ride?" Julianna blinked. If her sister had just told her she wanted to learn how to box at Gentleman Jackson's, Julianna couldn't have been more surprised. "Truly?"

"Yes." Mary's nod was resolute. She lifted her chin, and even though Julianna could see fear still lurking in Mary's eyes, she could tell that her sister was determined. Julianna knew from experience, whenever Mary became determined, nothing could sway her. That was one of the many things Julianna loved about her sister. She was brave when she chose to be. Brave and kind and wonderful.

Mary had good reason to be afraid of horses. Their father had put her atop one when she was far too young.

"Julianna was three years old when *she* learned to ride and she had no problem whatsoever," Papa liked to say whenever he was reminded of the fact that Mary had been mortified by her first attempt at riding. The little girl had been thrown from the pony, and while she'd landed on soft grass with only a few scrapes and bruises, she'd been terrified of horses ever since.

Father was right. Julianna *had* been three years old when she'd learned to ride, and she'd taken to it like a fish to water. But Julianna and Mary were quite different. Where Julianna had always been adventurous and full of energy, Mary had always been quiet and reserved and cautious. It was a mistake Papa had regretted for years and one that had cost her sister her ability to participate in many outings.

"Are you quite certain, dear?" Julianna couldn't help but ask.

"Yes," Mary replied, even though Julianna could feel her sister's hand trembling. "I was hoping you'd take me to the stables and ask one of the groomsmen to assist."

A slow smile spread across Julianna's face. "I think I know just the groomsman for the task."

"Mr. Worthy?" Mary replied with a coy smile.

"Precisely," Julianna replied with a nod.

THIS WAS GOING *to be fun*, Julianna thought an hour later as she and Mary marched down to the stables. Mary didn't own a riding habit, so she'd had to make do with one of Julianna's, which was too long in both the arms and skirt. Regardless, Julianna thought her younger sister looked adorable in the dark sapphire habit that one of the maids had quickly tailored so she wouldn't trip over it. The sleeves had simply been rolled up.

Mary had worn a pair of her own boots that weren't precisely riding boots. Julianna thought it best to match fit rather than function.

Rhys was in the far corner of the stables, helping the smithy to shoe one of the horses when they entered. He was using a hammer to beat the burning black metal into shape. Once again, his shirt was off—and Julianna had to glance away, swallowing hard, when he turned slightly and she saw his muscled abdomen. Was that a scar? She'd only seen it for a moment and certainly didn't want to be caught staring.

"Good morning, Mr. Worthy," she called when he'd finished his chore.

He turned and wiped sweat from his forehead, giving her his most outrageously charming smile. He knew *precisely* how inappropriate he was being, going about shirtless. He was making poor Mary blush.

"Ah, Lady Julianna, come for another tour? Bring anyone else with you? The Prince Regent, perhaps?" he asked with an unrepentant grin.

"Not yet," Lady Julianna replied. "Though I do hear he's arriving soon."

The house party had been agog at the news that both the Earl of Kendall and the prince would be arriving soon. Of course, Julianna found it laughable, given the fact that Kendall had already been serving them all in the dining room night after night. But given her promise to Worthington, she'd dutifully kept her mouth shut.

"Then what brings you out today?" Rhys asked. He no longer even pretended she wasn't here to bother him. That was interesting.

"Mary would like riding lessons," Julianna announced. "We were hoping you could assist."

"Riding lessons?" Rhys turned his attention to Mary. "Is that right?"

"Yes, Mr. Worthy," Mary said with a brave nod. "I've decided I must stop being such a ninny. Though I do hope you'll pick the tamest mount in the stables for me," she added, her voice cracking slightly.

"I know just the mare," Rhys replied. "And it would be my pleasure to help you, Lady Mary."

Mary smiled and wandered over to the other side of the blacksmith's area to get a closer look at the work he was doing.

"Let me clean up and I'll be right back." Rhys tossed a towel over his shoulder. As he passed Julianna he paused. "Here to attempt to make me quit again, are you?"

"I don't know what you mean." She stuck her nose in the air.

"Oh, so you don't intend to give me hell at every turn today?" he asked.

She did her best not to look at his glistening chest. "I expect you to give my sister proper riding lessons, if that's what you're getting at."

"And I suppose you'll be happy to provide me with constant corrections should my lessons not be to your liking?"

"If I must," she said with a dramatic sigh, before giving him a smug smile.

Rhys arched a brow at her and strode away toward the staircase at the far end of the stables.

Julianna joined her sister and she and Mary spent several minutes watching the blacksmith shoe the horse. Another one of the groomsmen came over to assist after Rhys left and the blacksmith used his tongs to dunk the shoe Rhys had hammered into a bucket of water to cool it before the groomsman helped to attach it to the horse's hoof with nails.

"It doesn't hurt the poor thing, does it, Anna?" Mary asked wincing.

"Not at all, dear," Julianna replied. "They don't feel a thing."

Mary expelled her breath. The poor young woman had probably been inside stables more during this house party than she'd ever been in her life. She didn't know the first thing about horses.

"What is all of that?" Mary asked next, turning toward the huge tack wall that covered one entire side of the building.

"That's the tack," Julianna replied, before spending the next several minutes pointing out items such as saddle blankets, pads, girths and cinches, martingales, stirrups, bridles, and reins.

"What's a martingale?" Mary asked just as Rhys came striding up behind them.

"It's a strap that's applied from the girth to the head piece," Rhys answered. "It's part of the harness that assists in the horse's head carriage."

Julianna turned at the sound of his voice. His hair was wet and slicked back and he was wearing new clothing. At least his white shirt was on and buttoned, but his skin-tight breeches left little to the imagination. He'd clearly just taken some sort of bath. No doubt he'd poured the wash bowl over his head and the water had sluiced down his muscled chest to— No. That line of thinking was not helpful. She needed to concentrate on why she was here. For Mary's riding lessons.

Of course, Julianna would never have asked Rhys to teach Mary if she thought he would be an unsuitable teacher for her sister. She'd seen him around horses enough during their courtship and since he'd been pretending to be a groomsman to know that he was quite knowledgeable. He was arrogant, of course, but something told her that he took Mary's concerns seriously. Julianna was confident that he would make this as painless as possible for her sister.

Rhys turned his full attention to Mary. He spoke to her in a calm, reassuring voice and he looked straight into her eyes. "Before I went upstairs, I asked Henry to saddle Whisper. She's the calmest horse in Lord Clayton's stables. I think you'll like her very much."

Mary only nodded, her eyes wide as tea saucers. "She certainly sounds as if she's the correct horse if one is judging on name alone."

Rhys laughed. "Precisely, my lady. Now, come with me."

Ignoring Julianna again, Rhys offered Mary his arm and led her out into the barnyard where Henry and Whisper were already standing.

Whisper was a beautiful sorrel mare, slight of stature, clearly with a tame and serene disposition. The horse stood quietly eating an apple out of Henry's hand.

"She doesn't look so frightening," Mary whispered, her throat working as she swallowed.

Julianna's heart ached for her sister. "Be brave," she called softly as Rhys escorted Mary over to meet the horse.

"First, you must be properly introduced," Rhys said. "Lady Mary, this is Whisper. Miss Whisper, this is Lady Mary."

The horse merely blinked her big doleful dark eyes at Mary.

"Nice to meet you." Mary's voice shook slightly as she performed a slight curtsy.

"Would you like to touch her?" Rhys offered Mary next.

Tears sprang to Julianna's eyes as she watched Mary reach out and softly pat Whisper on the head. Whisper stamped her hoof and continued to crunch her apple.

Mary retracted her hand, laughing softly. "She's lovely."

The horse pushed her muzzle under Mary's hand and Mary's delighted squeal made Julianna's heart clench.

"She likes you," Rhys said to Mary with a kind smile. "And I don't blame her."

"I don't blame her either," Henry added.

Mary blushed and glanced away from the young groomsman.

Julianna smiled. Whatever problems she'd had with Rhys in the past, he was being kind and patient with her sister and

116

that made her throat tight. He might be Detestable, but even she had to admit he wasn't *entirely* detestable. Not today at least. Not if he was being so good to Mary. Mary didn't deserve his ire, of course, but a lesser man would have taken his anger at Julianna out on her sister.

"You're not so bad at all," Mary said encouragingly to Whisper.

"Would ye like ta give her an apple, milady?" Henry asked Mary.

Mary glanced back at Julianna as if to ask for guidance.

Julianna nodded encouragingly. "Go ahead."

"As long as you're certain she won't bite me," Mary replied to Henry.

Henry placed a small apple in Mary's hand, and she squeezed her eyes shut and held her hand toward Whisper's mouth.

"It's all right," Rhys said, guiding Mary's hand closer. "She won't bite, I promise. Which is more than I can say for your sister."

Mary was obviously too worried about a potential bite from the horse to hear that little dig. She kept her eyes closed and her hand out. But Julianna heard it and she waited for Rhys to glance back at her before she gave him a smile that said *just wait till I get done with you.*

Whisper nibbled the apple out of Mary's hand and Mary's joyful laugh further delighted Julianna. She clasped her hands together. "You're not frightened, are you, Mary?" she called.

"Not at all," Mary replied, opening her eyes and staring in awe at the horse's large head. "It's a bit ticklish, if I'm honest."

Rhys laughed again. "It is, isn't it? Whisper loves apples. She's certain to favor you for giving her one."

"Good," Mary replied. "I can use all the goodwill I can get."

The horse finished with the apple and Mary dusted her gloves together before expelling her breath. "Must I climb up now?" she asked, pure dread apparent on her features.

Rhys chuckled. "No. No. We're not quite ready for that yet. First, it's important that you learn how to look after a horse before you attempt to ride one."

"Look after?" A frown wrinkled Mary's brow.

"That's right," Rhys replied. He took the reins from Henry and nodded at the groom to return to the stables.

Henry tipped his hat to Mary before he left. She blushed beautifully once again.

"He's a terrific one ta be teaching 'er, milady," Henry said to Julianna as he passed her on his way back into the stables.

Julianna shook her head. Yet another sycophant at the altar of the Duke of Worthington? Honestly, the man *had* to be paying these people to pretend they liked him as much as they did.

But when Julianna glanced back at Rhys, she had to admit that the way he continued to treat her sister was about to make her a proponent of a man she'd been calling Detestable for over a year.

"Before you can properly learn to ride," Rhys was saying to Mary in a steady, certain voice, "you must learn how horses behave. You must build a relationship with the animal."

"Is that why you had me pet her and feed her an apple, Mr. Worthy?" Mary asked, blinking up at him.

"Precisely," Rhys replied with a nod.

Julianna moved closer and watched as Rhys gestured to a small wooden table near the barn door. It had been laid with a variety of items that he obviously meant to use to teach Mary. "Taking care of a horse is every bit as important as riding," Rhys said. "It begins with grooming."

"I agree," Julianna added from behind them. "*Some* people

even tend to take better care of horse's feelings than people's feelings. Isn't that right, Mr. Worthy?"

"Perhaps that's because horses never give one a reason to be mistrustful, my lady," he replied without missing a beat.

Mary glanced back and forth between the two of them, frowning.

Next, Rhys picked up the comb. After showing Mary how to gently stroke through Whisper's mane, he let her try.

Mary's first attempt was a bit awkward but after a few moments, she dared a step closer to the horse and was able to comb her mane quite capably. "I'm terribly sorry, Whisper," Mary said to the horse. "I fear my maid is much better at arranging hair than I've ever been."

Both Rhys and Julianna laughed.

Next, Rhys moved on to leading. "I want you to help me walk Whisper out into the paddock," he said to Mary. "It will help to further build an affinity between the two of you."

"Affinity," Julianna called from her spot in the shade near the barn door. "That's often important between people, too, isn't it, Mr. Worthy? That is until one of them disappears for no reason."

"Affinity *is* important between people *and* horses, Lady Julianna," Rhys replied, the smile never leaving his face. "Especially affinity that lasts longer than it takes to say, find a new mount."

The look on Mary's face this time was downright dubious. Julianna ignored it and narrowed her eyes on Rhys. Bless it. The man had an answer for absolutely everything.

She watched with pride, however, as Mary led Whisper around the paddock, gently holding the lead and glancing back at Rhys every so often to ensure he was still close by. He nodded his assurance and gave her an encouraging smile.

"Now, we'll try tying," Rhys finally announced after they'd

spent a considerable length of time leading Whisper around the paddock.

"What'll we tie her to?" Mary asked, glancing about.

"The fence on the far side of the paddock," Rhys replied.

Mary dutifully trotted after him toward the fence.

"Are you coming, Lady Julianna?" Rhys called without looking back for her.

"No," Julianna called back. "I think I'll just remain here in the shade, if that's all right with you, Mary."

Mary nodded her assent.

"Are you certain, Lady Julianna?" Rhys replied. "You do realize I won't be able to hear your barbs from so far away?"

Mary glanced back at Julianna with a decidedly questioning frown on her face. Julianna shrugged. Poor Mary. No doubt her sister wondered why the deuce two people who had reportedly kissed only two days ago were trading digs with one another today.

"It's fine, Mr. Worthy," Julianna called back in a singsong voice. "I'll be certain to save the best barbs for your return."

Julianna waited in the hot barn for the better part of a half hour while Rhys and Mary took turns tying and untying Whisper from the fence.

By the time they returned to the stables, Mary leading Whisper, Julianna was feeling depleted and anything but ready to trade more barbs with Rhys.

"Did you see me, Anna? Did I do it correctly?" Mary asked, excitement evident in her voice.

"You did it perfectly, dear," Julianna replied, giving her sister a wide smile. "But it's getting late and we must get back to the house to dress for the picnic."

"You've made an excellent start this morning, my lady," Rhys said, taking the reins from Mary's hands.

"Thank you for your help today, Mr. Worthy," Mary replied. "I may not be able to ride yet, but I do feel ever so much more comfortable...at least around Whisper here." She reached out and stroked the horse's muzzle.

"That's how it works," Rhys replied. "One step at a time. I do hope you'll return. Next time, I'll show you how to saddle and mount."

"I'd like that," Mary replied with a sweet smile.

"You may even bring your sister back with you," he said, a grin still plastered on his face.

"Indeed." Julianna gave him a tight smile. "Next time I might teach *you* a thing or two, Mr. Worthy."

CHAPTER SEVENTEEN

The next morning, Rhys met his friends in the storage room of the servants' hall in the basement of the manor house. They'd begun meeting in the room ever since they'd been found talking in the library one day by one of the guests. As usual, Rhys was the last to arrive.

"Still in the game?" Bell asked the moment Rhys strode through the door.

"Yes, you?" he shot back, giving his friend a wide grin.

"Indeed," Bell replied. "Kendall is, too."

Rhys glanced at the earl. Kendall didn't say a word. "What's wrong with you?"

"Don't ask," Clayton said, waving his hand. "The poor chap was caught kissing Miss Wharton in the library earlier this morning."

"The devil, you say! Who found you?" Rhys asked, slapping his friend on the shoulder and laughing.

"We were *not* caught kissing," Kendall retorted, pulling his shoulder away. "We were *almost* caught kissing by Miss Wharton's lady's maid, Albina, and that is quite different."

"Oh, the lady's maid? You're fine then," Rhys replied with another laugh.

"I'm glad you think so," Kendall shot back, rolling his eyes.

"It's the *mother* you have to worry about," Rhys said with a wink.

"Agreed," Clayton replied with a nod.

"So, what's the news, chaps?" Rhys asked, rubbing his hands together. Ever since informing his friends that Lady Julianna had discovered him in the stables the first day of the house party, he'd yet to tell them he suspected she was trying to make him quit. He intended to mention Lady Julianna to them as little as possible.

"Well," Clayton replied, "in addition to Baron Wharton and the Prince Regent joining our little group on Monday, apparently the Marquess of Murdock will be arriving as well."

"Murdock?" Rhys's head snapped up. "What's *he* doing joining the party? I didn't know you were friendly with him, Clayton."

"I'm not, particularly," Clayton replied. "It was the strangest thing. He wrote me a letter. Apparently, the man cannot bear to be away from the company of his betrothed for so long. He's coming here to see Lady Julianna."

"Really?" Bell arched a brow. "That's...odd."

Rhys bit the inside of his cheek, but quickly ensured his normal devil-may-care smile appeared on his face. "Hard to believe, given that he's betrothed to Lady Julianna," he said with a snort.

"That's not all," Clayton continued, shaking his head. "Apparently, he's so enamored by her, he's written to the Duke of Montlake asking him if they might move up the wedding date."

"Really?" Bell drawled again, his eyes widening slightly.

"Sounds like Murdock cannot wait for his wedding night," Clayton continued with a chuckle.

Rhys clenched his jaw. Did Julianna know about this? She hadn't mentioned to him that her beloved Murdock was on the way. And she certainly hadn't mentioned that her wedding day had been moved up. But given the extent of their interactions in the stables, neither were exactly pieces of information he would expect her to be particularly forthcoming with.

Still, Rhys couldn't ignore the clench of his stomach when he'd heard that Murdock wanted the wedding date moved up. "Did Murdock mention a new date?" he heard himself asking.

Bell glanced at him with an arched brow. Rhys steadfastly ignored the marquess.

"No," Clayton replied. "But it sounded as if he wanted it to be as soon as possible."

"Apparently, Lady Julianna is remaining chaste until her wedding night," Bell replied, before adding, "Apologies, Worth. I hope that doesn't rub you the wrong way."

"It doesn't rub me the wrong way," Rhys replied, doing his best to keep the nonchalant grin on his face. "I wish Murdock the best. He's going to need all the help he can get, being married to that woman the rest of his life."

CHAPTER EIGHTEEN

This time Julianna didn't even pretend to sleep. It had to be close to midnight and she hadn't slept a wink. She was at the window in her and Mary's bedchamber, staring out at the moon again.

She loved to imagine all the other people underneath the moon, all the other lives that were unfolding beneath its calming steady light. There were so many people in the world. People who had much worse problems than she had, but she couldn't help sometimes staring up at the moon and wishing she could trade places with one of them. Perhaps live the life of a young woman who *didn't* have to meet her family's high expectations. The life of someone who was free to marry whomever she chose, and slump at the dinner table, and forget her manners from time to time, and wear clothing that was not of the latest fashion, with never a hair out of place. Sometimes when Julianna looked at the moon, she imagined a type of freedom that would never exist in her life, and if only for a few brief moments, she was happy.

"Can't sleep again?" came Mary's soft voice out of the darkness.

Julianna turned to her sister with a guilty look. Mary had lit a candle. "Oh, dear. I do hope I'm not keeping you awake."

"I never knew how much trouble you had sleeping," Mary replied, padding over to stand next to Julianna. They didn't have this problem at home. They had separate bedchambers across the corridor from each other.

"I don't usually..." Oh, who was she fooling? She'd had trouble sleeping for months and her sister might as well know it. She didn't need to put on an act for Mary. "It's been difficult for some time now," she said instead.

"Come, tell me about it," Mary offered. Taking the candle, she moved over to the two chairs near the fireplace and sat in one, motioning for Julianna to sit in the other. She placed the candle on the table between the chairs.

Julianna slowly followed her sister, trying to think of what she could possibly say to explain her recent troubles.

"What's the matter?" Mary asked as soon as Julianna was settled in the seat across from her. "How long have you been unable to sleep?"

Julianna took a deep breath. "I suppose it began after my engagement to Lord Murdock."

"Ah," Mary replied wisely. "That doesn't surprise me."

Julianna looked twice at her sister. "It doesn't? Why?"

Mary gave her a sympathetic look. "I didn't feel as if it was my place to say this before, but the truth is, I don't know that you and Lord Murdock suit."

"What?"

Mary winced. "I know. I'm sorry. Perhaps I shouldn't be saying it now either, but I've never got the impression that you were particularly happy with the match. *Lord Murdock* seems happy with the match. *Mama and Papa* seem happy with the match. But you never have. That's why I said what I said the other night, about not marrying someone you don't love."

Julianna opened her mouth to deny it but quickly shut it again. What good would a denial do? She'd been so accustomed to refuting her true feelings that the first words on the tip of her tongue had been an immediate denial. What did that say about her? What did that say about the role she was expected to play? "I don't know if I love him," she offered lamely, but truthfully.

The look Mary gave her was filled with both skepticism and empathy. "Don't you, Julianna?"

Julianna's eyes filled with tears. Why was something so obvious to her sister so difficult for her to admit? "I don't know. I...I don't think I am very happy about the wedding though," she allowed herself to admit. "That may be why I cannot sleep."

"How did it feel to say that?" Mary asked in a quiet, reassuring voice.

Julianna contemplated the question for a few moments before a truly happy smile spread across her face. She knew for certain it was the first time in months her smile had been genuine. "It felt good, actually. Quite good, if I'm honest."

Mary reached over and laid her hand atop Julianna's. "Anna, you've always been so good and dutiful. The perfect daughter in the perfect family. I've always admired you for it."

Tears stung the backs of Julianna's eyes again. "The last thing I feel is perfect. Lately I feel like I'm quite a mess."

Mary shook her head. "You're far from a mess, Anna. But you are only human. And I think you've gone about the last few years, at least the last few months, putting everyone else's desires ahead of your own."

"It feels wrong to do anything less," Julianna admitted.

"Anna, think about it. You kissed Mr. Worthy."

Julianna buried her face in her hands. "I know. I already told you I shouldn't have done that."

"No, no," Mary's voice was soft and forgiving. "I didn't mean that. I meant that you need to ask yourself why. I think it's because for the first time in your life, you're defying what's expected of you."

"Being rebellious, you mean?" Julianna asked with a half-hearted laugh.

"Yes, well, as rebellious as you and I will ever get, perhaps. But you're not happy. And kissing Mr. Worthy was a way to express that."

Bless it. If only her lovely, trusting little sister knew the whole truth.

"It does make some sense," Julianna allowed. "But you know as well as I do that Mama and Papa would be devastated if I called off my engagement to Lord Murdock."

Mary nodded sagely. "But consider that *you* might well be devastated if you don't."

Julianna squeezed her sister's hand. "It's not as if I can marry a groomsman."

"Perhaps not, but the fact that you can't keep from blushing when you're in Mr. Worthy's presence tells me a great deal."

"I do not blush around Mr. Worthy!" Julianna insisted.

A sly smile popped to Mary's lips. "Very well. If you say so. I'm certain your cheeks turn red for an entirely different reason around him, then."

Julianna shook her head and smiled. "I blush around Mr. Worthy?" she asked, scrunching up her nose. Oh, God. If that were true, she could only hope Rhys didn't notice. No. If he'd noticed, no doubt, he would have mentioned it to her by now.

"Yes," Mary confirmed, "even though you two have begun trading barbs, which, for the life of me, I don't understand."

"It's…complicated," Julianna replied, biting her lip. How could she possibly explain it to Mary?

"I only know that I've never seen you that way with a gentleman of the *ton*. It reminded me of the way you used to speak about the Duke of Wor..." Mary let her sentence trail off and pressed her lips together. "I'm sorry, Julianna. I didn't mean to mention Detestable."

Julianna patted her sister's hand. Mary was such a dear. She was always thinking about other people's feelings. Here she was at this house party to look for a potential match for herself and instead she was worried about Julianna's match with Murdock, and how she appeared to be enamored of a groomsman.

"At least the wedding's not till spring," Julianna replied with a sigh. "I have plenty of time to contemplate the matter. I expect it will all feel better to me after a bit of time passes."

Mary gave her a dubious glance. "I don't think that's how it works, Anna."

"You let me worry about Lord Murdock and Mr. Worthy," Julianna said, shaking away the unsettling thoughts of her upcoming wedding. They'd spent long enough talking about her, at any rate. "You should be much more interested in finding a match. At dinner tonight, did you speak with Lord Mixton again about going for a ride?"

Mary shook her head. "I'm not certain I'm brave enough yet. I need another riding lesson. Do you think Mr. Worthy would be up to the task?"

CHAPTER NINETEEN

R hys couldn't help his smile when Julianna and Mary arrived at the stables early the next morning. Julianna might be a thorn in his side at the moment, but the woman was nothing if not determined.

"I didn't think you'd be awake at this hour, Mr. Worthy." Julianna called in the sweet voice he'd come to recognize as the one she liked to use when she was pretending to be nothing more than a house guest with a penchant for visiting the stables every chance she got.

"And I didn't think your tongue would be so sharp this early, Lady Julianna," he replied in his most accommodating groomsman-like tone. "I suppose we both must suffer being wrong."

Mary crossed her arms over her chest and glanced back and forth between the two of them before shaking her head. "Mr. Worthy, I was hoping you'd do me the favor of providing me with another riding lesson."

Rhys turned his full attention to Mary and bowed. "Lady Mary, I'd like nothing more," he said with all the sincerity he truly felt. He was nothing but pleased that Lady Mary had seen fit to allow him to continue with her lessons. It meant that she trusted him, and there could be no greater compliment for a trainer than that.

"I'll just go get Whisper saddled," he called to her.

Lady Mary nodded.

Rhys gave Julianna a tight grin. "Don't miss me too much, my lady."

"I'll *try* not to," she replied in tone that dripped with sarcasm.

Was he missing his guess, or were they *enjoying* ribbing each other at this point? He had to admit, he found himself looking forward to her next verbal jab and coming up with his riposte. He whistled to himself as he headed toward Whisper's stall.

Minutes later, Rhys returned with Whisper, but he hadn't yet saddled the horse. "I thought I'd show you how to prepare her for a ride," he said, smiling at Mary.

Mary returned his smile. "I'd like that very much."

While Julianna stood silently nearby, Rhys showed Mary the proper way to put the blanket on the horse's back and then the proper way to fit and fasten the sidesaddle.

"Of course, given the number of servants your father no doubt employs," Rhys said. "I realize you will not be doing much of your own saddling, Lady Mary, but a proper horsewoman understands the fundamentals of such things in case she is ever called upon to know them in a difficult situation."

"I agree with you completely," Julianna said.

Rhys eyed her carefully, waiting for the additional snide comment that was certain to follow. When she merely blinked at him innocently, he continued, "Anyone I teach will be prepared for all eventualities."

"I see," Julianna replied. "Like perhaps the eventuality that you up and leave in the middle of a lesson, never to be heard from for, say, months?"

Ah, there it was. Over Mary's head, Rhys gave Julianna a tight smile.

For her part, Mary gave Julianna a quelling glance. "Why would you ask that, Anna?" Then she turned to Rhys, "You're not planning to leave, are you, Mr. Worthy?"

"Not at all, Mary," Rhys replied. "*You're* not the type of young lady one leaves."

Nearly growling, Julianna ground her boot into the dirt. She was most likely imagining it was his face. Ha.

Once the saddle had been properly fitted and Rhys had helped a slightly trembling Mary atop it, he spent the next hour leading her gently around the paddock while Mary clung to the reins, her knee firmly ensconced around the horn.

Julianna, of course, took advantage of every opportunity to exasperate him.

When they walked past her and Rhys said, "Keep your back straight and your shoulders centered—the horse can tell when you're not confident." Julianna said, "Yes, listen to him, Mary. Mr. Worthy here is a master at confidence. Some might even say *arrogance.*"

When they trotted past and Rhys said, "If you lean forward, the horse can guess what you want," Julianna replied with, "Yes, and Mr. Worthy is an expert at knowing what ladies want."

And when they came by at a slow canter and Rhys said, "Just let me know when you're tired and we can take a small break," Julianna didn't miss a beat when she shot back, "Don't listen to him, Anna. I happen to know Mr. Worthy doesn't know what a *small break* is."

"What does *that* mean?" Mary asked, frowning.

"Yes," Rhys said. "What *does* that mean, my lady?" He blinked innocently at Julianna.

"Oh, nothing," she said to Mary, ignoring Rhys. "I'm sorry. Please continue with your lesson."

Mary shook her head and promptly returned to clutching at the saddle for dear life. It wasn't until they'd been at their lesson for the better part of two hours that Mary announced that she thought she might be able to ride about the paddock alone for the first time and Rhys happily obliged. He waited in the center, watching her like a mother hen and its chick for several rounds before he strolled over toward the barn door to stand next to Julianna.

"She's truly getting the hang of it," Rhys said.

"She is. You've done an excellent job teaching her," Julianna replied, not looking at him.

"What was that?" He cupped a hand behind his ear.

"I believe you heard me." But her smile belied the tone of her words.

"Praise? Words I never thought I'd hear coming from you, Lady Julianna."

"She looks good, Rhys. I appreciate your...help."

"Why, Lady Julianna, are you trying to *thank* me?" He batted his eyelashes at her.

She let out a long sigh and turned to face him. "Whatever else I may think of you, I happen to adore my sister, and she's been scared witless of horses her whole life. That is until you helped her. She was thrown at the age of three." Julianna shook her head slightly as if to dispel the unwanted tears that sprang to the backs of her eyes.

Rhys's throat tightened. He searched Julianna's face. "I didn't know she'd been thrown, and at such a young age. I'm sorry to hear that."

Julianna shrugged. "Not exactly something one mentions when one is courting."

"No, of course not," he replied. "But it certainly explains why she is so fearful. I don't blame her." He leaned back against the barn wall and stared out to watch Mary and Whisper.

"She's had a difficult time of it," Julianna continued. "Especially growing up in a household where the rest of us love horses so much."

Rhys inclined his head. "I can imagine. I only hope I've been able to help her in some small way."

A slight smile flitted across Julianna's lips. "She couldn't stop talking about the progress she made yesterday. She was quite proud of herself."

"She should be proud. She's done a fine job of over-coming her fear," Rhys continued.

"Do you think she requires another lesson?" Julianna asked, crossing her arms over her chest.

"That depends," Rhys replied evenly. "Will you have time for more lessons after Lord Murdock arrives?"

Frowning, Julianna's arms fell to her sides and she turned to face Rhys, her mouth slightly open. "Lord Murdock? What do you mean?" She eyed Rhys warily.

Rhys shrugged. "Clayton told me he's arriving tomorrow."

"Tomorrow?" Julianna shook her head. Her frown intensified.

"You didn't know?"

"I...ah, didn't know what day it would be," she replied, tugging at the collar of her riding habit.

"I see," Rhys replied, just before the devil on his shoulder prodded him to say more. "I hear your wedding date is being moved up to autumn, as well. I suppose best wishes are in order."

"My *what*?" Julianna's tone increased nearly two octaves.

Rhys nodded nonchalantly. "Clayton mentioned that

Murdock wrote to your father to ask him to agree to move up the date. Surely, you knew *that.*"

Julianna pressed her palm to her chest as if she couldn't breathe. "Mary," she called, in a frantic-sounding voice. "I think that's enough for the day. We must get back to the house. I have a letter to write."

CHAPTER TWENTY

Early that afternoon, Rhys was still working in the stables. He wiped away the sweat dripping from his brow with the back of his sleeve. He stabbed more hay with his pitchfork and tossed it onto the heap at the back end of the empty stall in which he stood.

He'd been spending his days cleaning tack, bailing hay, mucking stalls, and grooming horses. Things he'd helped the stablemaster at Worthington Manor do when he was younger, but things he hadn't done in years until now.

As a duke, he spent his days waking at noon, meeting briefly with his solicitor, drinking, gambling, and enjoying the finer things in life until well into the early morning hours. Then he fell into an exhausted slumber before doing it all over again the next day.

His time spent here working in Clayton's stables was the first in years that he'd actually felt…useful. Teaching Mary Montgomery to ride yesterday had been one of the most satisfying things he'd done since he could remember.

The poor young woman had obviously been frightened to death of horses, and while he couldn't imagine being fright-

136

ened of the animals he so loved, he could imagine how difficult it must be for her to live around the large creatures and be uncomfortable. It must have been torturous for her all these years.

Horses were some of the gentlest mammals in the world, and he'd known just the right horse in Clayton's stables to use with a frightened rider. Whisper had been kind and still and relaxed, the perfect mount for Lady Mary.

When Julianna had first arrived at the stables yesterday with her sister in tow, Rhys had been convinced she was back to cause him more trouble. And indeed, she'd done her best to rile him by sniping at him at nearly every turn. But he could tell that she was truly worried about her sister's fear of horses and her ability to ride.

Mary seemed like the type of young woman who wouldn't step upon an ant. She was friendly and caring and had a true smile for everyone. The opposite of her sister, he thought with some chagrin. He briefly wondered if Kendall had met Mary Montgomery.

Rhys had done something good yesterday. He'd helped Lady Mary take the first steps toward conquering her fear of horses and riding. She was a brave young woman. He hoped he'd be able to help her again before the house party ended.

If Julianna was still attempting to get him to quit his position, she wasn't doing a particularly adept job of it. All she'd managed to do was come out here every day and cause him a bit of work. Little did she know he was relishing work these days.

She didn't expect him to enjoy work. Neither did his friends. After all, they'd bet him that he wouldn't be able to make it two weeks performing the duties of a true servant. Perhaps they'd have been right had he been confined to the stuffiness of the house with its proper etiquette and formal attire, but here in the stables, where he could sweat and work with horses, Rhys was in his element.

Horses, after all, didn't expect anything of you other than food and water and hay and kindness. Horses didn't care if you were a duke. Horses didn't care what the *Times* said about you and whether you were supposedly a drunken, moneyless lout.

The members of the *ton* had no idea he'd purposely chosen his reputation. They'd no idea that he'd picked his public image right down to the fact that Hollister's was the most infamous of the gaming clubs and he'd be certain to get the most attention for his drunken, gambling loutishness if he spent his leisure hours there, rather than one of the famously discreet gentlemen's clubs like White's or Boodle's. They'd no idea that he lost great sums at Hollister's in order to cultivate the image that he was in debt.

Then he'd go to an even more discreet club. The type of gambling hell few gentlemen of the *ton* even knew about, and there, there, he *won* large fortunes. Enough to have more than quadrupled the amount his father had left.

But even with that carefully fostered reputation, Julianna had still been interested in him. At the time he'd been lulled into thinking it was because they actually had things in common, like a love of horses and a robust sense of humor. At some point, he'd decided that his title was obviously more important to her than his reputation for drinking and gambling.

Rhys had been convinced that it showed how little Julianna cared who she married, as long as the title was prestigious. Murdock was second in line. And Murdock wasn't known for anything much, certainly not being a drunken lout. He was as dull as dishwater as far as Rhys was concerned. He'd met the man a time or two, but didn't remember much about either encounter.

The devil on his shoulder had made Rhys mention Murdock's arrival to Julianna. He couldn't help but wonder if she already knew. And Rhys had got his answer. She hadn't known. She clearly hadn't known that her *fiancé* was arriving tomorrow, and she almost certainly hadn't known that he'd asked to move up the wedding date. Neither fact had seemed to be welcome to her. *That* was interesting.

Murdock would soon be sharing a wedding night with Julianna. The thought flashed unbidden into Rhys's mind. He wanted nothing more than to vanquish it, but it sat there, taunting him, angering him. For a reason he couldn't define and didn't want to examine.

He stabbed another forkful of hay and tossed it. Damn it. That unwanted thought led to the next, which was a memory that haunted him upon more occasions that he cared to admit. The memory of Julianna in his study one night well over a year ago.

As was customary when courting, Rhys had invited Julianna and her parents to his house for dinner one evening that Season. He spared no expense, consulting with both his housekeeper and butler on the details including the china, the cutlery, the meal, even the candles. Only the best beeswax for Lady Julianna's visit.

He ensured the dining room was filled with her favorite flowers, lilacs. He produced a bouquet for both her and her mother.

The dinner had progressed as well as could be expected, with Lord Montlake glowering at him and Lady Montlake lavishing him with nothing but praise—the couple were on opposite sides of the issue when it came to the question of whether Rhys would make a good spouse for their beloved eldest daughter.

At one point, Julianna excused herself to use the privy and she was gone longer than any of them expected. Her mother was begin-

ning to worry and was about to go in search of her daughter, when Rhys volunteered. He knew the house the best, of course. It only stood to reason that he should go in search of a guest who may have lost her way.

After searching the route to and from the privy with no luck, he found her minutes later in his study, of all places. She was standing near the window looking up at the moon.

"There you are," he said, stepping inside the nearly dark room. Only one candle on the desktop and the glow of the moon through the window illuminated the space.

Julianna guiltily turned with a start and dropped the handkerchief she was holding to the floor. Ever the gentleman, Rhys came over to pick it up for her, and discovered it was one of his own, monogrammed with his initials. It had obviously been sitting on his desk. He handed it back to her.

"Thank you," she said quietly. "I wanted it because..." She pulled it up to her nose. "It smells like you," she admitted, a sheepish smile on her lips.

"Keep it," he breathed, reaching out and pushing a lock of her soft blond hair from her forehead.

"Is Mama getting worried about me?" she asked, wincing.

"Yes," he answered, "we should get back." He turned, expecting her to come with him back to the dining room.

"Can't we keep them waiting just a bit longer?" she breathed.

He turned again to see a mischievous gleam in her eyes.

Rhys arched a brow. "What did you have in mind, my lady?"

She took a step forward, rose up on her tiptoes, and put her arms around his neck. She looked up at him with those beautiful light-green eyes that would tempt a saint and said, "I was hoping for our first kiss."

And he obliged her, by God. Standing there, smelling the scent of her perfume, the moonlight filtering through the window, he'd pulled her into his arms, lowered his mouth to hers and kissed her.

The kiss had soon transformed into much more. They were

unable to keep their hands from each other. He'd lifted her into his arms and lowered her onto the chaise in the corner. Then he lowered himself atop her, grinding his hips against hers, wanting her unlike he'd ever wanted any woman in his life.

Julianna's hands were in his hair; she helped him to quickly divest himself of his coat, while his mouth never left hers, then she helped him to pull up her skirts while his hand skimmed along her calf, her thigh, until he found the apex between her legs.

She reached down and cupped him beneath his breeches. He groaned and tried to move his hips away, but she wouldn't let him, stroking him until he'd nearly come in his clothing.

He'd finally wrenched her hand away to set his breathing back to rights before he touched the delicate spot between her legs. She'd moaned and moved closer to his hand. When his finger entered her, her hips nearly came off the chaise. He wanted to bury himself inside her and pump his hips slowly, rubbing her until she called his name, and then following her into sweet oblivion.

But Julianna deserved more than a quick shagging on a chaise in his study. She deserved a wedding night worthy of a princess. And he intended to give her one. But here, on his chaise, he could give her something to remember him by.

Using his thumb, he flicked at the nub between her legs, again and again as he watched the expression of amazement play across her expressive features. She was so wet, so hot, so ready for him. He gritted his teeth against the agony of his erection, determined to make her feel pleasure tonight with no such reciprocation for him.

Julianna's head moved back and forth fitfully on the cushion beneath her and she made tiny little gasping sounds in the back of her throat that made Rhys even harder. He continued to flick that aching spot until she grabbed at his upper arms. "Rhys," she cried. "What is happening?"

"Just let go," he instructed her, leaning down and whispering in her ear. "Don't be frightened."

He continued to whisper to her telling her how much he wanted *her, how beautiful she was, and finally, how much he wanted to watch her pleasure, until her legs tensed and she cried out softly, her breaths coming in hard, sharp pants as her entire body shook.*

He carefully helped her to right her clothing and sit up as she continued to breathe heavily and looked at him through confused, glazy green eyes that were wide with—dare he guess?—wonder.

"I've never felt anything like that before," she whispered.

He leaned forward and kissed her forehead. "That's how it will always be between us, Love," he promised.

Her mother had called from the corridor then, and Rhys had hastily replaced his jacket before helping Julianna to stand. They'd made some asinine excuse about looking at the artwork that hung over his desk, but he was fairly certain Lady Montlake suspected they'd been doing something quite different from appreciating a painting. She hadn't said a word, however.

THE REST of the story was history. He'd left soon after. God, he'd come so close to making the biggest mistake of his life. Looking back, Rhys could see precisely how big a fool he'd been. Julianna had been the one to initiate the kiss in his study, just as she had that day at the tree line. He'd been the one who stopped it in his study. If it had gone too far, she could have roped him into marriage. He'd have been trapped and she'd have got precisely what she wanted.

But if she were trying to trap him, why had she been the one who'd stopped it at the tree line?

Rhys stabbed the hay with even more vigor; again and again he flung the straw into the opposite pile. His muscles would ache in the morning. Hell, they ached now. No amount of physical labor would cause the memories of her to fade. Worse. No amount of physical labor would cause the *doubt* to fade.

Because *what if* she wasn't an actress? *What if* she had only ever loved him, and had been devastated that he hadn't come back that Season, and had been forced to make another match? It wasn't as if he could have expected her to wait forever. He'd wanted her to be happy. *What if* she was telling the truth and the story in the *Times* had simply confused the issue?

He stopped pitching and stood staring unseeing at the stall door, his breaths exhaling in deep bursts. What if he was the biggest horse's arse to ever live?

CHAPTER TWENTY-ONE

Julianna made her way over to the window and pulled back the curtain enough to pick out the stables across the meadow. She and Mary had just finished lunch with their mother and had been bidden to rest. Julianna had no more interest in doing so than usual.

Rhys had told her that Lord Murdock was coming. Had Rhys merely been trying to provoke her, or was it true? And if it *was* true, why was that the first she'd heard of it?

But Murdock's visit wasn't what had truly alarmed her. For some reason, the possibility of his attempt to move up the wedding date had nearly sent her into a panic. She'd written a letter to Papa, asking if it were true.

Meanwhile, her mother had confirmed that Murdock did, indeed, intend to arrive in the morning.

"I thought you knew, dear," was all Mama had said in response to Julianna's questioning. "Your father wrote and told me."

But Julianna hadn't known, and it irked her that her

father or Murdock wouldn't think to tell *her* such a thing. It seemed like a common courtesy.

Julianna traced the cool windowpane with her fingertip. It was difficult to think of Murdock when Rhys was so near. Rhys had surprised her again today. Perhaps as much as her sister had. He'd been patient, kind, and caring while teaching Mary to ride. He'd gone out of his way to ensure Mary was comfortable and he'd been willing to stop the lesson each time she appeared overwhelmed. Julianna's heart had been in her throat watching them together in the paddock.

Rhys had taken her barbs in stride, actually. Apparently, nothing ruffled the man. Julianna had been counting on the fact that he was a pampered, privileged duke who was used to being waited on, not waiting upon. Surely, doing a hard day's work and being critiqued at it would cause such a man to become frustrated and ill-tempered. Instead he appeared to have endless patience with both Mary and the horse. Surprising indeed.

Sighing, Julianna crossed her arms over her chest and contemplated the entire complicated affair for a moment. Perhaps she'd been thinking about this all wrong. *Perhaps* he hadn't left and tossed her over on a whim. *Perhaps* the ladies' gossip on the tour was true and Rhys was deep in debt. *Perhaps* he had wanted to be responsible, and hadn't wanted to bring a wife into that situation. *Perhaps* he *was* a hard worker and a kind man who merely wanted to help her sister learn to ride and win his bet to put his outrageous gambling debts to right. *Perhaps* he had truly loved her, and it had hurt him when he'd seen that story in the *Times*, making him believe that she'd never cared a whit about him. *Perhaps* the past was in the past and she no longer needed petty revenge.

Julianna rushed over to her wardrobe to find a riding habit. She had to get to the stables and talk to Rhys.

~

Less than an hour later, Julianna made her way to the stables with tentative steps. A riot of emotions ran through her and she was still mentally jumping from thought to thought in a matter of seconds. For the first time in an age, she felt as if the sadness and anger that constantly plagued her whenever she thought of Rhys Sheffield had lifted.

Apparently, Rhys was destitute. No doubt that was why he hadn't wanted to offer for her. He'd said something about doing her a favor. That could easily have been what he meant. And if that were true, she could see how he had truly felt as if he *was* doing her a favor by leaving and not returning. It would have been kinder, of course, to tell her the truth. But men like Rhys were proud. She tried to imagine her own dignified father having to admit to gambling away his fortune. The thought made tears spring to her eyes.

If Rhys had left to allow her the space to move on, however, he should have been resigned to seeing her engagement announcement in the paper. Only it hadn't *just* been her engagement announcement. No. It had included a bit of nonsense the *Times* had invented about her setting her sights on the *next* most eligible bachelor. Which of course made Rhys think that she had only been interested in him for his title.

Only, the story in the *Times* hadn't been *entirely* made up. Per her mother's directive, Julianna *had* set her sights on the next most eligible bachelor. It was just that she'd truly been falling in love with Rhys before he'd left. Oh, the whole thing was so complicated. How would she and Rhys ever be of the same mind on the matter?

But now she realized where they'd both been wrong. She'd been trying to exact revenge and he'd been trying to hold onto his indignation. Perhaps they didn't need to forgive each other. Perhaps they didn't even need to forget. Perhaps they merely needed to…call a truce.

And that's why she wanted to speak to him, to tell Rhys that she'd decided to leave him be. To wish him luck on winning his bet, and to assure him that however preposterous she might think it, she had no intention of telling anyone about the three noblemen pretending to be servants at this house party.

She found Rhys in Violet's stall, combing her mane and speaking gently to the lovely mare.

"Be careful," Julianna said with a grin, leaning over the rail. "You'll spoil her for all other males."

Rhys turned to look at her and returned her grin. "That's my intention," he replied.

Julianna swallowed. Were they talking about Violet any longer? She shook her head to clear the tension in the air and quickly changed the subject. "You'll see I'm quite proper again today with my riding habit. No more riding astride." She stood back so he could see the garnet red habit she wore.

"A pity," he murmured, not removing his gaze from hers.

Heat rushed between her legs. She had to change the subject again, quickly. "I saw your friend, Kendall, this morning. He was carrying logs to the library."

Rhys shrugged and went back to combing Violet's mane. "Seems footmen get the worst chores. Kendall's poking around fireplaces while I get to attend to the lovely Lady Violet here."

Julianna stepped back up to the railing and rested her arms atop it. "None of you have been recognized yet, I presume."

"Not as of this morning," Rhys replied with a laugh. "I still have every intention of winning, however."

"I've yet to see Lord Bellingham," Julianna added.

"I doubt you'll see Bell unless he wants to be seen."

Julianna laughed. "Tell me. Has Lord Kendall found a potential bride?"

Rhys turned to her. "I suspect he fancies Miss Wharton, but don't you dare tell him I said that." He winked at her.

"Miss Wharton?" Julianna replied, lifting her brows. "She seems to have a fine head on her shoulders. However, I fear Sir Reginald has his sights set on her already."

"Fine head on her shoulders?" Rhys scoffed. "I heard she made a scene at dinner the first night."

"Oh, she did," Julianna replied with a laugh. "But I suspect she only did that to rid herself of Sir Reginald's company. I thought it was quite a marvelous idea, actually. Wish I'd thought of it myself."

"Hmm. Perhaps there's more to Miss Wharton than meets the eye," Rhys replied, slowly nodding.

"I think so," Julianna said with a nod of her own. "Mary quite likes her also."

Rhys finished combing Violet, opened the stall door, and came out. Julianna tried to ignore how handsome he was in his groomsman's attire. There was something about him in that casual white shirt and breeches that made her mouth go dry.

He dusted off his hands against his firm backside. "Have you come for another ride, my lady? Or are you simply here to torture me again? I won't give up easily, you know."

Once again, Julianna wondered what precisely they were talking about. Rhys's words were loaded on so many levels.

"While I do enjoy torturing you," she replied with a grin. "I came here specifically to ask if we might declare a truce." There. The words were out.

He arched a brow. "Truce?"

"That's right." She nodded. "Which, of course, means I promise to keep your secret for the remainder of the house party."

"In that case, how can I say no?"

"Excellent," Julianna replied. "But I would love it if you'd still allow me to come out here each day until I leave, in order to ride Violet or Alabaster. I do so love to ride."

He inclined his head toward her. "I'm certainly not going to keep you from it. You are an excellent rider, Julianna." His tone was soft, conciliatory.

"Will you ride with me? Be my groomsman?" she asked, allowing the hint of a coy smile to touch her lips.

His eyes widened. "It would be my pleasure, my lady." He bowed to her.

"Excellent," she repeated. "There is just one more thing I wanted to say."

"What's that?" he asked nonchalantly as he walked over to the tack wall.

Julianna cleared her throat. "Thank you again, for helping Mary."

Rhys turned to face her and bowed. "My pleasure, my lady. I'm more than willing to provide another lesson at any time."

Julianna nodded. "Thank you. We may just take you up on that."

"Or if you can't think of another way to make me quit my position as groomsman, perhaps you'd like to meet me at the archery targets across the lawn and take direct shots at me."

She couldn't help her surprised smile that quickly turned into a laugh. "Have I been that awful?"

He returned her smile. "Well, you did give me fair warning at the start. I believe you said you intended to enjoy every moment, including ordering me about yourself."

"Yes, well, I can't say it hasn't been fun, either, but..." She met his gaze. The smile slid from her face. "I am truly thankful, Rhys, for your making the lessons so painless, for Mary's sake."

He nodded once. "I hope you know that whatever disagreements you and I have had, I would never take it out on a nervous young rider or her horse."

"I do know that," Julianna replied simply, then she shook her head to clear the sudden intimacy, the sudden gratitude she felt for him.

"You must admit I've impressed you with my ability to work so diligently, haven't I?" His grin was unrepentant.

She laughed. "Perhaps."

"And you've impressed me with your ability to doggedly pursue someone," he added.

"Thank you," she said with another laugh. "I do appreciate that." She turned toward the front of the stables. "Well, I should get back. Mama will be looking for me."

"Wait. One last thing."

She turned back halfway. "Yes?"

Rhys clapped his hands together. "I believe a truce between the two of *us* calls for a celebration."

She arched a brow. "What did you have in mind?"

"Meet me at the lake at four o'clock. I'll bring the wine."

CHAPTER TWENTY-TWO

Later that afternoon, when Rhys galloped up to the edge of the lake on horseback, Violet was already there, tied to a post near where Julianna and Mary had had their picnic several days earlier.

Rhys quickly dismounted Alabaster and tied him next to Violet, then he unbuckled the basket he'd attached to the back of the saddle and slung it over his forearm, before making his way down to the water's edge to meet Julianna.

She was sitting on a blanket under a willow tree. The meadow behind them was obscured by a tall hedgerow and more trees. She'd picked the most private spot imaginable.

He grinned at her as he joined her and set the basket next to them.

"Wine?" she asked, arching a brow.

"Of course. And a few other things." He grinned at her.

Julianna sat up and dug into the basket. She pulled out a bottle of red wine, part of a wheel of cheese, some bread, and some grapes.

"I thought you might be hungry," Rhys said.

"This looks like the perfect meal for a truce celebration.

Especially the wine." She rummaged around in the basket a bit longer. "But where are the glasses?"

"Glasses!" Rhys snapped his fingers and then pressed his palm to his forehead. "I knew I forgot something."

"It's all right," Julianna replied with a laugh. "We'll make do."

Rhys set about uncorking the wine and then tossed the cork back into the basket. "You drink first," he offered, handing her the bottle.

"Yes, we'll share," she replied, a mischievous gleam in her eyes. "After all, we have kissed before. We might as well not pretend as if we haven't. And sharing a bottle is far less intimate." She took a long swig from the bottle.

"You have a point," Rhys replied, taking the bottle from her hand and enjoying his own long swig.

TWENTY MINUTES LATER, they were halfway done with the bottle and lying side-by-side on the soft blanket staring up at the clouds between the willow tree's branches.

"What's your favorite place on the property?" he asked her.

"The hill beyond the paddock," she replied without hesitation. "I like to go there and sit and watch the horses run."

"Are you serious?" he asked, blinking.

"Yes, why?"

"Because that's *my* favorite spot. I didn't know anyone else liked it there."

"It's so calm and peaceful there. I love watching the horses," she explained. "They don't care about things like manners or looks."

"Looks?" he asked, surprise in his tone.

Julianna sighed. "Yes. Have you any idea what it's like to

be told your entire life that your beauty is the only important thing about you?"

"No," he replied quietly. "But I do know what it's like to be told your title is the most important thing."

There was a pause before Julianna replied, "I suppose we have something in common then." She leaned up momentarily and took another drink.

Rhys stared up at the clouds. He felt like an ass. He'd never stopped to consider the fact that debutantes had pressures of their own.

"Would you believe me if I told you I've often had the thought that I like horses better than people because they don't expect anything of you?" he asked.

"Yes!" she exclaimed, lifting a hand into the air. "They don't care how you dress or how you behave or even who your family is."

"Agreed."

She leaned up and gave him a sheepish grin. "Would you believe me if I told you that was one of the reasons I liked you…when we were courting?" she clarified.

"I didn't care who your family was?" he replied with a laugh.

"Well, perhaps you did. But I always felt as if I could be myself around you. As if I didn't have to be perfect. I've never felt that way around anyone. Especially any gentlemen of the *ton*. I've only ever felt that way around horses."

Rhys's chest tightened. He sat up, handed her the bottle, and studied her face. "The truth is, Julianna, I always felt the same way about you."

Perhaps it was the wine or the fact that they'd finally declared a truce, but they were speaking to each other the way they had when they were courting, and it felt both real and inexplicably comforting.

Julianna glanced away. "I've been having trouble sleeping."

"You too?" he asked, taking yet another swig from the wine bottle.

"Yes. And I normally sleep like the dead," Julianna admitted. "Why do you think *you* can't sleep?" She, too, took another drink.

"I cannot make my mind stop thinking, I suppose," he answered, sitting up too.

"It's funny how everything has worked out," Julianna said, leaning back against her braced wrist on the blanket.

"I suppose funny is one word for it," Rhys replied with a sigh.

"May I ask you a question?" Julianna said.

"You just did." He laughed and took another swig from the bottle.

She batted playfully at his hand. "Don't drink it all." She pulled the bottle from him and took another long sip. "And I would like to ask you *another* question, if you please."

He grinned at her. "Very well, go ahead."

"You never did tell me, but I still want to know. Why did you leave?" She bit her lip hesitantly. "Why did you go to the country that spring?"

Rhys took a long swig from the bottle and then expelled his breath. He hung his head. He supposed it was finally time to tell her the truth.

"I didn't go to the country," he said quietly.

"What?" She searched his face, shook her head. "What are you talking about? You lied?"

"I had to. At the time I wasn't at liberty to say where I was going."

She shook her head again. "I don't understand."

He met her gaze. "I went to France."

Julianna gasped. She sat up straight and pushed away the

154

nearly empty wine bottle. "France?" She peered at him as if trying to discern from the look on his face whether he was jesting.

"That's right," Rhys continued, pushing his hair back from his face.

"Why in the world would you go to France? We're at war with France."

He chuckled softly. "Yes, I'm well aware. That's why I went."

"You went to France to fight Napoleon?" she breathed, her eyes widening as if she couldn't quite believe it.

"No, I went to France to *spy* on Napoleon. Well, his men, not Napoleon himself," Rhys clarified.

"You're a spy?" Her eyes were so wide Rhys saw the whites.

He shook his head. "Not exactly. I was sort of doing a favor for a spy. Helping the Home Office if you will."

"Oh," she said knowingly. "You were helping Lord Bellingham."

"I wouldn't say that exactly...but I wouldn't *not* say it," Rhys replied with a grin. "When one is in need of an unlikely spy, who better than that drunken lout, the Duke of Worthington?" His voice was filled with irony.

She reached over and touched his knee. "Are you a drunken lout?"

"No, but if one has a false reputation, one might as well use it to one's advantage. Or one's country's advantage, as the case may be." He grinned at her, retrieved the bottle and took another sip before offering the final sip to her.

Julianna took the bottle and stared at him. "How long were you gone?"

He took a deep breath. He might as well tell her the entire truth. "I was only in France for six weeks. But that's why I didn't ask you to marry me before I left. I knew I would be in danger, and I didn't want you to have to mourn for me if I didn't come back."

Julianna stared down at the blanket for a few moments, apparently lost in thought. The sound that came out of her mouth was part sigh, part cry. "It was too late for that," she finally said softly. "But if you were only gone for six weeks, why *didn't* you come back?" She lifted her head again. Her brow was furrowed. "Why did you wait so long to write?"

Perhaps it was the wine or the sultry afternoon or the devil who seemed to *live* on his shoulder, but Rhys's next words were, "Let me show you." He leaned forward, untied his neckcloth and tossed it aside, then pulled his shirt entirely over his head with both hands at the neck.

Julianna sucked in her breath sharply. Her gaze roved over his bare chest. She swallowed, hard.

Rhys straightened his shoulders and pointed to a scar on his lower abdomen, partially covered by the waist of his breeches.

"Here," he said. "Here is where I was shot. The second time."

"No!" she exclaimed. She peered at it. "I thought I saw something like this one day when you had your shirt off in the stables. But I couldn't be certain." She leaned even closer. "Oh, God," she said quietly, her hand over her mouth. "What happened?"

Rhys tossed the crumpled-up shirt toward the basket. "I was at a dinner party in Paris and was betrayed. By someone in our ranks."

She searched his face, her own turning pale. "Who?"

"We don't know who yet. But we suspect it's the same man who betrayed our army at Bidassoa."

She clapped her hand over her mouth again. "No!"

"I'm afraid it's true. And believe me when I say that as

soon as we hunt down the bastard who's responsible for this, his life won't be worth a farthing."

"Did you...did you nearly die?" She gulped.

"Yes, but amazingly not from this gun shot, or the other one."

"The other one?" Her mouth formed a wide O.

"The other one tore through my thigh. Quite bloody. I still have a slight limp."

"I haven't noticed," she breathed.

"It gets worse when I'm tired or have walked a great distance," Rhys admitted.

Julianna's eyes shimmered with tears. "If the two shots didn't nearly kill you, what did?"

Rhys stared past her into the distance, his mind focusing on that awful night. "When I was shot, first in the thigh, then in the abdomen, I was standing on a balcony. The force of the second shot sent me over the railing."

Tears slid down both of Julianna's cheeks. She shook her head silently.

"Thankfully, I was only on the second floor. But it was far enough. I don't recall much after that. They tell me I was unconscious for two months." He shook his head and refocused his gaze upon her.

She looked down at the blanket and shook her head as if trying to make sense of the incredible things he'd just told her. She closed her eyes. "That's why you didn't write," she murmured.

"Yes, and when I finally woke up..." He swallowed hard this time. It was more difficult to say the words than he ever would have imagined.

She opened her eyes and swiped at her tears with the backs of her hands. "What happened Rhys? Why didn't you come back?"

He met her gaze. "When I finally woke up...I was...blind."

Julianna silently hugged her knees, rocking back and forth, while tears continued to drip down her face.

"It's true," Rhys continued, swallowing the lump of fear and guilt and doubt that had formed in his throat. "I was blind, and I didn't want you to feel obligated to commit to a blind man."

She lifted her head to meet his gaze again. "I wouldn't have tossed you over, you must know that."

"Yes, but would you have loved me? Would you have wanted me?" The words somehow made it through his dry throat.

"Yes, yes of course." Tears streamed down her cheeks now.

He pressed his lips together. "You say that, but you can't really *know*, Julianna."

She searched his face, her eyes red from crying. She pressed a hand to her chest. "You don't believe me?"

"I want to, Julianna. Truly I do." He'd never meant words more. Never been more ashamed of the truth.

Her tears stopped. They were quickly replaced by anger. She clenched her jaw. "I'd given you no reason not to trust me. Why did you send me that awful letter?"

"I..." His voice faltered. "I felt as if I had no choice. I wanted you to be free to marry a whole man."

Julianna staggered to her feet. "I feel more betrayed by that admission than I did by that hideous letter. Why, Rhys? *Why* can't you trust me?"

He stood too and clasped her hands in his, searching her face. "You don't know how difficult it is for me to trust. I wish to hell I wasn't that way, but I am."

"Why? Tell me why, damn you!" She wrenched one wrist from his grasp.

He let her other wrist go and expelled his breath, rubbing his forehead where a headache had begun to form. "My father always told me I'd only be wanted for my title. I felt... Julianna, when I met you, I felt as if I had actually met someone who might love me for me."

Her brow crumpled. She searched his face. "And after you went blind, you decided that wasn't true? I still don't understand. *Why?*"

"The truth is..." He glanced away. Hating himself for every word he was about to say. "I think I was too cowardly to learn the truth. I couldn't have stood it if you had rejected me."

She took a deep breath, closed her eyes again briefly and nodded. Then she shook her head. "So you didn't even give me the chance."

He nodded.

Wiping away a fresh set of tears, Julianna lowered herself back onto the blanket. She took a deep breath. "When did you regain your sight?" she asked quietly.

Rhys resumed his seat beside her again. "Not until this past April, after you were engaged."

"So that's why you decided to write me the letter telling me you hoped I hadn't thought too much of our acquaintance."

He nodded. "Until then, I hadn't decided what I would say to you. I dictated it to my valet."

"That explains the handwriting," she said with a humorless laugh.

"Did he do a poor job of it?"

"It didn't seem like you," she said, shaking her head slowly.

Rhys clenched his hand into a fist against the blanket. "I hated dictating that letter. But I couldn't let you go on thinking you cared for a blind man."

She searched his face. "I *did* care for a blind man, Rhys. Don't you understand?"

He glanced away. "I expected you to be angry, hate me even, but then when my valet read the paper to me that day last spring, the column that mentioned how you'd set your sights on Murdock because you'd failed with me, I was convinced you'd only ever cared about my title."

"You were wrong, Rhys. And so was the meaningless paper." Her words sounded angry, but there was also an underlying tone of resignation. And perhaps sadness.

It tore at him. He met her gaze again. "I know that now, Julianna, but what's done is done. For what it's worth, however, I am truly sorry."

Julianna lifted a hand and reached over to touch his bare shoulder. "Rhys? Things might have been so different between us, if only—" She stopped and shook her head. "I wish…"

He leaned forward and pressed his forehead to hers. "Don't say it, Julianna."

"I must say it."

He kissed her gently, closing his eyes, knowing the words that she was about to say would rip through his heart.

"I wish," she hung her head, "things had been different. I wish…I'd known."

He took a deep steadying breath. There would be no better time to ask her what he needed to know. "Now that I've told you, you must tell *me* something, Julianna. I need the truth."

She cupped his face in her hands and nodded. "Of course. Anything."

Guilt tore at him. He'd often told himself these many months that Bell had saved him from Julianna's schemes by offering him the chance to go to France. The thought had plagued Rhys for so long, he had to finally know the truth. He took a deep breath. "That night, in my study two years ago, were you trying to seduce me to trap me into marriage?"

Her hands fell away from his face and she pulled back. The look of indignation mixed with anger on her face immediately told him he'd made a grave mistake. Her eyes blazed. Her chest rose and fell, her cheeks turning red before she finally spat, "You fool, you utter fool. Do you honestly believe I would do that? Is that what you think of me?"

Julianna pushed herself to her feet again and shook her head, looking down at him with a mixture of pity and disgust in her gaze. Her hands were clenched into fists at her sides. "You still don't trust me. After all this time, even the time we've spent together here, you still believe I only ever wanted you for your title and your fortune."

"Julianna, I—"

"Let me speak!" she demanded. "The truth is that I know you're destitute, and if you'd stop and use your brain for a moment, you'd realize that my trying to seduce you that night makes absolutely no sense. If I had been trying to trap you into marriage, I could have easily told my parents how far we truly *did* go, and my father would have demanded you do the right thing then and there. If I was after your proposal at all costs, as you say, why didn't I do that?"

"Julianna," he cried, "please."

She swiped tears from her eyes, eyes that were still blazing with outrage. "I'll tell you why, because I truly thought we were falling in love and that you intended to ask me to marry you because you *wanted* me, because you *loved* me. That is why, you complete horse's arse!"

And with that, she stomped off the blanket, past the willow, and around the hedgerow—and Rhys was left knowing just how wrong he'd always been.

CHAPTER TWENTY-THREE

The next night at dinner in Lord Clayton's large dining room, Julianna was seated next to Lord Murdock, who had arrived that afternoon. There were at least two other new guests at the dinner table that evening. Baron Winfield, Frances Wharton's father, and the Prince Regent himself, who'd come based on Sir Reginald's invitation.

The rumor was that Sir Reginald intended to announce his engagement to Miss Wharton that evening. Julianna kept glancing over at poor Miss Wharton. The young lady looked positively miserable. Miss Wharton kept exchanging glances with the Earl of Kendall, who everyone was talking about, but still no one noticed was serving the table dressed as a footman. Watching that play out was by far the most interesting part of the meal.

Meanwhile, Julianna could not stop thinking of her afternoon at the lake with Rhys yesterday. She'd thought about it all night last night, even begged off going to dinner because of it. She'd thought about it all day today as well. Mary had tried to talk to her, but Julianna hadn't been ready to talk.

She wanted to forget the entire discussion. She wanted to forget him. Forget that he was still in the stables, pretending to be a groomsman. Bless it, how she wanted to forget everything. But each time she tried to think of something else, like Lord Murdock's imminent visit, she found herself drawn back to thoughts of Rhys. He'd nearly died. He'd been blinded. Both things were too awful to contemplate.

He lied to her.

After she'd been faithful and waited for him.

But *he* didn't trust *her*.

No wonder he liked horses so much—he resembled one's hindquarters.

"Julianna," her mother whispered from her side at Lord Clayton's dining table. "You're not smiling."

Julianna shook her head and forced a smile back onto her face. She'd tried this evening to concentrate on what Lord Murdock was saying, but each time she leaned toward him, a memory of Rhys with his shirt off, lying on the blanket under the willow tree, flashed through her mind.

Mary's words came back to haunt her. Julianna had pushed the thought away ever since that night. "I don't think you should marry someone whom you don't love," her sister had said. But what had love to do with their world? No. Julianna needed to do what she always should have done, concentrate on her future. And her future obviously lay with her marriage to Lord Murdock.

She glanced at the marquess and gave him another tentative smile. The truth was, she and Murdock had done little more than exchange smiles so far this evening, and the smiles were beginning to make her cheeks ache. She'd already decided that after dinner, she would ask to speak to him privately to discuss their future. She still didn't like the fact that he'd decided to arrive at the house party without telling her. And if the rumor about moving up the wedding date was true, she'd have a few choice words for him.

The dinner seemed to drag interminably. The only conversation she and Murdock managed were a few pleasantries about his journey from London and a variety of comments about the meal itself. Had he always been this dull? She hadn't noticed before. But now that she thought on it, she hadn't spent *that* much time in his company. They'd danced at balls, he'd brought her punch, they'd shared one meal at her father's town house and one meal at Murdock's town house, and then he'd asked her to marry him and she'd said yes, and they hadn't seen much of each other since, honestly.

When Sir Reginald stood to make his announcement, Julianna was glad only because it broke up the monotony. But when Lord Kendall climbed up to the sideboard, ripped off his powdered wig, and declared himself to Frances Wharton, the entire dining room was agog. Within minutes, Lord Kendall and Sir Reginald were arguing, and Miss Wharton had fled the room.

Julianna turned to Murdock. "It looks as if dinner has unceremoniously ended. Would you care to go to one of the drawing rooms so we may speak privately?"

Murdock nodded, stood, and helped pull back her chair. They managed to flee in the midst of the commotion. Julianna doubted they'd be missed. She leaned down to whisper her plans to her mother and Mary so they wouldn't worry.

Once outside the dining room, Murdock led the way down the corridor and around a corner until they came to a row of drawing rooms near the front of the house. They chose the first door they came to. The empty room was covered in shades of dark blue and gold.

Julianna remained standing. Murdock offered her a drink, which she declined.

"Well, *that* was something," Murdock said. He'd gone to the window and was staring out across the darkened front drive of the estate. "Why in the world do you think Kendall was pretending to be a footman?"

Julianna stared at Murdock's profile. He was handsome, to be certain, with dark-blond hair and brown eyes. He was fit and tall and had good teeth. But he never seemed to be silently laughing about things the way…Worthington was. In fact, Murdock seemed to take everything a bit too seriously.

She didn't really know him, she reminded herself. Perhaps if she talked to him more, she might learn what he found humorous.

"It seems awfully romantic that Lord Kendall interrupted Miss Wharton's engagement announcement," she offered.

"Romantic?" Murdock scoffed. "It was an embarrassment. The poor young woman won't live down that humiliation for years."

"You think so?" Julianna replied, her brow furrowed. "I was thinking I'd like it if a gentleman wanted to marry me so much that he was willing to stand up on a sideboard to declare himself."

Murdock's nose wrinkled with disgust. "He made a fool of himself and Miss Wharton, if you ask me."

"You wouldn't declare yourself on a sideboard for me?" Julianna asked, her tone jesting, a smile on her face.

"Don't be absurd," Murdock replied, his lip curled in a frown. "I wouldn't disrespect you that way." He tugged at his coat and smoothed his hand down the front.

Julianna's face fell. So much for a sense of humor.

"Tell me," she said next. She strolled over toward the window to stand near him. "What do you find humorous?"

"Humorous?" His brows lifted. He seemed surprised by the question. "What do you mean?"

"I mean…what sort of thing makes you laugh?" she asked, watching him hopefully.

He furrowed his brow and seemed to think for several moments before lifting his head and saying, "Ah, I thought of something. Once when I was in an archery tournament at school, I took a step back and stepped on one of the arrows."

"Yes?" Julianna prompted, eagerly waiting for the humorous part. "Then what happened?"

Murdock's frown deepened. "That was it. I *broke* the thing in half. Must have laughed for five entire minutes. I mean what sort of an oaf *steps* on an arrow that he *needs*? Clumsy of me, don't you agree?"

Julianna wrinkled her nose and nodded. Very well, perhaps Lord Murdock wasn't particularly humorous, but he must have other qualities.

"You like horses, don't you?" she asked next.

Murdock shrugged. "They get you from one place to the next I suppose. Necessary evils."

"Evils?" she repeated, frowning again.

"Can't say they smell particularly good, and they cost a *fortune* to house and feed and take care of."

She eyed him cautiously. "You don't like to ride?"

"Oh, it's pleasant enough." He waved his hand in the air as if dismissing the topic.

"Do you know anything about the Godolphin Arabians?" she ventured.

"Horses?" This time he frowned.

"Yes, famous horses," she prompted.

"Why would I want to know anything about them?" He shook his head, looking a bit perturbed at her for asking. "They don't exactly teach you such things at *Cambridge*." He laughed uproariously at *that*, for some inexplicable reason.

Julianna expelled her breath. Something told her that if she continued down this path, she would find herself more disappointed. She might as well bring up the subject that she'd asked him here to discuss.

She folded her hands together carefully and took a deep breath. "Is it true that you asked my father to move up our wedding date?"

Murdock blinked at her. "Who told you that?"

"Uh...I heard it through Lord Clayton." There, that was somewhat true.

"I see. I didn't realize Clayton was in the habit of repeating things in *private* letters." Murdock seemed angry again.

"I didn't know you were coming here, either," she replied, a bit put off by the fact that instead of admitting what he'd done, he was blaming Lord Clayton for her finding out about it.

"I wanted to surprise you, my dear," he said, but the word *dear* sounded flat and unemotional. It made her uncomfortable.

She tried to smile, but the muscles in her cheeks wouldn't cooperate. "I don't understand why you couldn't wait to see me back in London."

He lifted both brows. "You don't want to see me?" His tone sounded hurt.

"I didn't say that." Bless it. This conversation was taking a turn for the worse. She needed to get back to the point. "I merely wondered why you'd choose to try to move up the wedding without asking *me* first."

His bark of laugher bounced off the windowpane. "I didn't realize I needed *your* permission."

Julianna's brows shot up. "Pardon?" He hadn't truly just said that, had he? In her family, her parents were well aware of the roles they each played, but her father never did anything without consulting with her mother first. It was a sign of respect as far as Julianna was concerned, and she knew her parents felt the same way about it.

"It would have been a nice courtesy," Julianna continued, doing her best not to grit her teeth. "Am I to have no say in our wedding plans? Besides, Father will simply discuss it with Mother who will discuss it with me."

"Well, *that's* quite unusual," Murdock replied, tugging at his coat again. His tone had turned imperious.

Julianna blinked. "What is?"

"A duke asking his *wife* for permission," came Murdock's pompous reply.

Julianna crossed her arms over her chest. "He doesn't ask for permission. He asks for her *opinion*. I see nothing wrong with that."

"I suppose that's one way to describe it." Murdock's tone had turned icy.

In addition to her folded arms, Julianna began to tap her slipper upon the rug. "Well, I would like to be informed of any changes to the wedding date. We'd planned it for spring, and I think it's best to keep it there."

She didn't want to vocalize the feeling of impending doom that clutched at her chest each time she thought of the wedding date being moved up. The truth was, the fact that it seemed so far off in the future was the reason she'd been feeling good about it till now. The moment she contemplated it happening in a matter of a few short weeks' time, her heart began to pound, and she felt as if she couldn't breathe.

Murdock's frown returned. "We'll see." He reached out and patted her shoulder, giving her a complacent smile.

Anger shot through Julianna's veins. He was clearly trying to placate her. Was this the sort of marriage they would have? One where he patted her and gave her a false smile and she had no say in anything?

"Yes," Julianna replied, returning his fake-sweet smile with one of her own. "We *will* see."

CHAPTER TWENTY-FOUR

Yet again, Julianna couldn't sleep that night. She tossed and turned, replaying the entire conversation with Lord Murdock in her head. She didn't even know who he was. She'd been so wrapped up in her mother's advice to ensure she fulfilled her destiny and became betrothed to the next most eligible man in the *ton*, she hadn't even stopped to consider whether she *wanted* to be married to him.

It had all been so easy with Rhys. She'd just assumed it would be easy with any man of her choosing. Murdock met all the measurements after all. He was tall, handsome, well-educated, wealthy, from a good family, possessed of a fine title. He had even been approved by both of her parents, which was something she'd never been able to say for the Duke of Worthington.

But somehow, she was just now getting around to realizing that those things didn't necessarily mean that her marriage would be a pleasant one. Her time with Rhys had been so different. They'd gone riding, talked, laughed about things, and even kissed (and more) in his study. He'd fulfilled all of the measurements as well (save for Papa's general disapproval).

But with Rhys, those things weren't what had made her like him so much. He'd actually been smart and funny and good company. She was beginning to fear that not only was Murdock neither funny nor good company, he showed signs of being domineering and arrogant. Rhys was arrogant too, of course, but in a charming way. Not in a way in which she wanted to strangle him, as she'd been tempted to with Lord Murdock in the drawing room earlier.

She needed to get away and think. She could not stay in this house one more day and pretend to be the perfect little debutante. Especially not when Lord Murdock would be following her around, smiling at her. She had no interest in playacting at the moment. She had to leave.

Dawn had barely broken over the horizon when she marched down to the stables to ask for a mount. Rhys was nowhere to be seen—and for that, for once, she was grateful. She didn't want anyone to know where she was going today. She wanted privacy and the chance to think about everything without interruption.

She asked for Alabaster. The steed would be the perfect horse to ride far and fast across the estate. To take her away from the niceties and the pleasantries and all the fake platitudes she was so sick of.

When Henry, the groomsman, brought Alabaster around, he said, "Are ye certain ye don't want an escort, me lady? Seems ta me Lord Clayton and Mr. Hereford won't like it if I let ye go alone."

"I'm certain, Henry. And if anyone comes looking for me, please tell them I insisted upon being alone. I'll be back late this afternoon."

Henry nodded, but his eyes were filled with doubt. "I'll tell 'em, me lady. But ye may want ta make it a shorter ride. It smells like rain in the air. If a storm's a brewin', ye won't want ta be caught out in it."

"You let me worry about that, Henry. Thank you for your help." She tossed him a coin, spun the horse around, and took off at a gallop.

CHAPTER TWENTY-FIVE

ater that morning, Rhys was mucking a stall when a commotion near the front of the stables caught his attention. A lady's voice was raised, and a small group of stablehands were gathered around her. It sounded as if they were attempting to calm her down.

At first Rhys wondered if it was Julianna. She seemed to be the most frequent lady visitor to the stables lately. But the longer he listened, the more he realized it was an older woman speaking. He recognized the voice, too, but he couldn't quite place it.

Rhys set down his brush and left the stall, dusting off his hands as he went. When he rounded the corner, it was just as he suspected. Three of the groomsmen and Mr. Hereford were gathered around a woman who was nearly hysterical.

"Don't worry, me lady," Henry was saying. "I'm certain she'll be back any moment now."

The woman to whom they were speaking was considerably shorter than the rest of them and Rhys had to wait for the circle of men to shift before he saw that the woman was…the Duchess of Montlake. Julianna's mother.

Rhys quickly ducked into the nearest empty stall to keep listening while ensuring that the duchess didn't see him. She might well recognize him, even though he was dressed in a white shirt and plain cloth breeches.

"Where did she go?" Lady Montlake nearly shouted.

"I don't know," Henry replied. "She just asked for a mount. She insisted upon going alone."

"And you let her, you fool?" Lady Montlake sounded as if she was about to cry.

Rhys narrowed his eyes on the scene. There were two possibilities. Either Lady Mary had arrived and asked to take Whisper out on a trot around the paddock, and the horse had got away from her (which seemed unlikely) or...

"I brought her Alabaster and she took off right quick," Henry continued.

Or Lady Julianna had come for a mount and left, and now her mother was worried because a nasty-looking storm was brewing. The sky had turned an ominous shade of dark gray, bordering upon black, and the wind had whipped up enough to knock over some small tables in the paddock.

Based on Henry's last words, Rhys knew the latter had happened.

"We'll send a party out ta look fer 'er," Mr. Hereford was saying. He began shouting orders to groomsmen and stable-hands to mount up.

Rhys didn't wait to hear more. He'd already gone in search of the second fastest mount in the barn. Clayton's second Arabian, Midnight.

He had the horse saddled and was flying out the back doors of the stables by the time they'd finally convinced Lady Montlake to calm down and allow them to search for her daughter.

CHAPTER TWENTY-SIX

She wasn't at the pond. She wasn't at the lake. She wasn't even on the hillside by the paddock, and he'd already scoured every part of the stables and barns for her. No, Julianna had taken off somewhere on Alabaster, and he needed to find her before this storm broke.

Acting on instinct, he turned from the lake and spurred his mount in the direction of the far end of the property, just as fat raindrops began to splash his hat and shoulders. He had to find her quickly.

By the time Rhys made it around the copse of trees near the edge of the forest and pulled Midnight up short, the rain was lashing him in wave after wave. The black skies had opened, and a deluge had begun.

He could barely see the outline of the gamekeeper's cottage through the cloud of rain. When he got close enough to make out the front door, he could also see that the door to the small barn next to the cottage was slightly ajar.

He rode Midnight up to the barn, jumped down, and pulled open the door. He quickly led the horse inside.

Despite it being mid-morning, the barn was nearly dark. Flashes of lightning were his only light.

Rhys expelled his pent-up breath. There, in one of only two small stalls, was Alabaster, his saddle and blanket removed, busily chomping on fresh hay.

Rhys quickly settled Midnight into the adjoining stall, removing his tack and providing him with a meal as well.

Then, bracing himself against the wind, Rhys braved the elements again. After closing the barn door, he sprinted across the slick grass to the cottage porch. He banged on the door with his fist, but didn't wait for an answer before swinging open the door and barging inside.

Julianna's head snapped to face him. She was sitting in a pile of blankets on the floor in front of a roaring fireplace. The fireplace and a few random candles blinking around the room were the only light.

"Rhys?" Her face was filled with confusion. "What are you doing here?" She had to raise her voice to be heard over the roaring wind and the rain.

"Looking for you. Your mother's worried sick," he shouted back.

"You're soaked." She eyed him up and down.

Rhys glanced down at himself. His shirt was plastered to his chest and his breeches left even less to the imagination than usual. He discarded his water-logged hat. Then he stamped his feet on the rug in front of the door before taking a seat on a nearby stool to remove his drenched boots.

Julianna clambered up from the pile of blankets and went immediately into the small bedchamber that adjoined the main room. He could see her shuffling around in the wardrobe before she returned carrying a dry white shirt, no doubt belonging to the gamekeeper.

"Here, take this," she commanded, tossing the shirt to

him. Then she returned to the pile of blankets and pulled a fur from the heap.

Rhys caught the shirt in one hand. He'd finished removing his boots and quickly pulled his wet shirt over his head, before Julianna handed him the fur, which he used to dry off as best he could before pulling the dry shirt over his head.

The shirt was smaller than his own, but it was dry and clean, and at the moment, that was all that mattered.

Rhys wrapped the fur around his waist and Julianna offered him a spot on the pile of blankets. "Would you like some tea? I made some," she offered.

He nodded. Now that he'd found her, he wasn't entirely certain what to say to her. They could hardly leave for the stables again, given the current weather conditions.

Moments later, she returned from the small kitchen with a steaming mug in her hands. She handed it to him, and he gratefully took it. She sat down beside him, and they were both silent for several minutes while he sipped.

"How did you find me?" she finally asked. The wind and rain were still whipping outside, but now that they were closer together, he could hear her better.

"I guessed."

She nodded. "Is Alabaster safe in the barn?"

"Yes, he's fine. He's with Midnight now."

"They're both excellent horses," Julianna replied. "I would have never forgiven myself if Alabaster had been hurt in the storm. I wasn't entirely certain where I was going today. I'd been riding around for a while before I remembered this place. I managed to make it here before the storm broke."

"I'm glad to hear that. Alabaster is quite special to Clayton and not just because of his lineage. Clayton credits him with his marriage. If it weren't for that horse, Clayton might still be a bachelor," Rhys said with a wry chuckle.

Julianna stared into the fire and nodded. "Yes, Lady Clayton told me the story. Quite a tale."

"Quite a way to become leg-shackled," Rhys replied, taking another sip from his mug.

The smile faded from Julianna's face. "I didn't mean to frighten Mama. I just had to get away."

"Away from what?" Rhys asked, narrowing his eyes on her.

Julianna shook her head and stared down at her hands that were clasped in her lap. "Away from my life."

He set the mug in front of the fireplace. "What happened?"

"Nothing." She paused for a moment. "And everything." She let out a loud sigh.

Rhys nodded slowly. "Well, I seem to recall the last time I saw you, you called me a horse's arse, but I'm willing to listen if you want to talk."

Julianna appeared to contemplate the offer for a moment. She rubbed her forehead with one knuckle. "I just thought...I thought it would all be easier, you know?"

"What would be easier?" he prompted, studying her face.

She shrugged. "Falling in love. Getting married."

Rhys continued to search her face. "Love? Are you in love with Murdock?" Why did his heart feel as if it would beat out of his chest as he awaited her answer?

"I want to be," she admitted, glancing away. "But I'm not. And he said some things to me last night that make me think I may never be able to love him."

Besides the surge of relief at her words, Rhys couldn't help the surge of protectiveness that also rose inside him. "Like what?"

"Like he didn't think it was any of my concern if he moved up the wedding."

Rhys inclined his head. "Not particularly charming of him."

"And that he thought it odd that my father asks my mother's opinion of things."

Rhys winced. "Oof."

She nodded.

Rhys took a deep breath. Rain splashed the windows and the wind howled. "For what it's worth, Julianna, I'm sorry I wasn't the man you needed me to be."

She met his gaze and lifted her chin. Tears shimmered on her eyelashes. "Are you sorry you didn't tell me the truth about your injuries?"

He'd had all night to think about it. Sleep had been no closer to arriving last night than it had for days. "Yes, I'm sorry I didn't tell you. Call it my pride—I simply thought you wouldn't want me any longer."

"You were wrong. I had feelings for you and when you left, I...felt as if you'd simply abandoned me."

He began to reach for her and then stopped himself, letting his hand drop back into the pile of blankets. "I never considered how it all must have made you feel."

"I understand now," she replied. "You weren't even aware for two months, and then you were blind. It's selfish of me to expect you to have been thinking of me at a time like that."

"But I should have, Julianna. I realize that now. I should have written the moment I woke up, to let you know what had happened. I thought I was being noble. I thought I was being selfless. Now I realize I was just being a horse's arse." He gave her wry smile.

She lowered her chin to her chest and expelled her breath. "I suppose there's no sense in regretting the past. As you said, what's done is done."

He nodded slowly. He couldn't argue with her. There was nothing left to say.

"Even if we wanted things to be different," Julianna continued. "There's no way my father would allow me to cry off."

Rhys swallowed the guilt and shame that had lodged in his throat. "No, Julianna. You couldn't leave him for me. Even if your father would allow it. It would be the wrong thing to do." A vision of Lady Emily Foswell's face floated through his mind.

"I know, Rhys. I know."

He reached out and cupped her cheek, sliding his thumb across her smooth skin. "The one thing that's never changed is how much I want you."

Julianna lifted her chin. Their eyes met and Rhys leaned forward, closer, closer, until his lips brushed against hers. It was soft, chaste; a kiss between two people who both wished they'd done things differently.

And then the kiss shifted.

Rhys's tongue tentatively explored the line between her lips, and she opened to him. He pulled her into his arms as their tongues met and a groan sounded deep in the back of his throat. He pushed up the skirts on her yellow riding habit and she wrapped her legs around his waist, sitting atop his lap.

Rhys tried to steady his breathing. Dear God. This was wrong and they both knew it, but if Julianna was to be consigned to a life of unhappiness married to a man she didn't love, Rhys could give her one afternoon of passion, if that was what she wanted.

His hands were in her hair and her hands were wrapped firmly around his neck. His mouth trailed to her ear, her neck, her *décolletage*. Her fingers worked at the buttons of the shirt he'd put on only minutes earlier, and she pulled it over his head.

His fingers worked at the buttons of her habit, which were undone in a matter of seconds. He gently leaned forward, so she would fall back on the heap of blankets. He helped her to pull off her habit and then she was clad only in her shift and stockings.

She quickly divested herself of the shift too and Rhys sucked in his breath.

"Julianna," he breathed, "you're gorgeous." His eyes traveled from the tips of her toes, up her long, slender legs and soft thatch of slightly darker curls between her legs, her flat belly, her perfect, full breasts. His gaze came to rest on her beautiful face.

"Kiss me, Rhys," she begged.

He divested himself of his breeches and she gasped when she first saw him. He didn't want to frighten her with his nudity. He quickly covered her with his body and pulled one of the furs over both of them to keep them warm.

The storm continued to rage outside, while Rhys took his time exploring every part of Julianna. First, he kissed her lips again, long and languidly, savoring the taste of her, the feel of her naked beneath him.

Then he lowered his mouth to her neck and nuzzled her, licked the shell of her ear. Her body bucked beneath him. He moved even lower. Cupping her full breasts in his hands, he lavished the attention of his tongue on first one, then the other. He sucked a nipple into his mouth and flicked it back and forth with his tongue. Her head was thrown back and her hands were moving of their own accord through his hair.

When he lowered his mouth even farther and began kissing between her breasts and then down her abdomen, Julianna's belly tensed. Her hands clutched his shoulders and her legs spread as he settled himself between them.

The first lick made Julianna moan. He cradled her hips in

his hands and pushed his tongue against her sweet core again. Her fingertips dug into his shoulders. He used the tip of his tongue to nudge at the spot between her legs that he knew would give her maximum pleasure. She moaned again.

He sucked the sensitive little nub into his mouth and flicked it ruthlessly with his tongue.

"Rhys," Julianna called. Her hands had left his shoulders to tangle in his hair once more.

He licked her again and again until her hips lifted off the blankets and he held her there, his hands cupping her warm buttocks while his mouth continued its gentle assault on her most intimate spot.

His tongue flicked her again and again until her legs tensed, and she cried out a final time before sinking back down into the blankets, her body trembling.

Rhys emerged from under the fur with an arrogant smile on his face. "How did you enjoy that, my lady?" he asked in his most Mister-Worthy-the-groomsman voice.

Her eyes weren't focused. She was staring blindly at the ceiling, the back of one arm splayed across her forehead, a look of wonder on her face. "There...are...no...words," she managed in between attempting to take deep breaths.

He wrapped his arms around her waist and pulled her tight against him, kissing the top of her head.

Julianna waited until her breathing returned to normal before she tugged out of his arms, tossed the fur over her head and began her own descent down his nude body.

"What are you doing?" Rhys asked, simultaneously alarmed and extremely aroused.

"What do you think I'm doing?" came her muffled reply.

She kissed his shoulders and his chest. She lightly raked her fingernails down his muscled abdomen, then she trailed her tongue along the line of hair that disappeared between his legs.

"I've been forced to look at your chest almost daily," she said, her husky voice still slightly muffled under the fur. "You don't know how much I've wanted to taste you."

Rhys was so hard, he ached.

He took a deep, steadying breath. He knew he would need to stop her at some point, but he couldn't help but wonder what she'd do if he allowed her to continue. In the end, his curiosity and his erection won.

He settled back against the pile of furs while Julianna's warm wet lips trailed down his abdomen. He could feel her hesitancy as soon as she reached his cock. Her hands rested on his hips. She kissed his tip and it twitched.

That's when he began to breathe heavily. "Julianna, you don't have to—"

Whatever words he'd been about to say were lost when she took him into her hot mouth. She sucked him, moving her tongue up and down. Oh, God, she was doing to him what he'd done to her. Damn. She was a fast learner too.

His hands fumbled beneath the fur. He was intent upon pulling her back up to kiss him. But when her mouth slid down the length of him, his hands fell uselessly to his sides. "Jesus Christ," he breathed.

He felt her smile against his thigh. "I take it you liked that?" came her slightly amused voice.

"Mmm hmm," he finally managed to murmur. His eyes were squeezed shut and his hips arched up as her mouth continued to slide up and down him.

She was torturing him. None of his fantasies had been this good. She pulled her lips from him and licked his tip again, sucking on just the end before taking his entire cock deep into her throat. She did it again and again until he was mindless, his hips thrashing, his hands tangling in her long, silken hair.

"Julianna," he breathed.

He couldn't do it. He couldn't make her his. Not after the heartache he'd caused her. It wouldn't be fair to her. It wouldn't be fair to Murdock.

He let her suck him until he was on the edge. His balls tensed. His fists clenched. He let her lick him one last time before he reached down and pulled her up to him in one fell swoop, kissing her deeply, his tongue driving into her mouth the way he wished his cock could drive into her wet warmth as he came against her hip.

His body shuddered and his pressed his forehead hard against hers, his breath coming out in short, hard pants.

"Rhys, I—" Julianna pulled the fur aside to look down at what he'd done. "I wanted you to make love to me." Disappointment sounded in her tone.

"I can't, Julianna," he breathed, trying to pull her back into his arms. "You know that."

"Why?" Anger mixed with the disappointment this time.

Still breathing heavily, Rhys forced himself to roll to the side, silently cursing himself with every breath. Somewhere in the back of his consciousness, he was aware that the storm had broken and the sun was shining through the windows again. He pushed away the covers, stood, and padded into the kitchen where he dipped a towel in a bucket of water and returned to Julianna's side.

Silently, he wiped his seed from her skin. "I'm sorry, Julianna. I shouldn't have done that."

Julianna pulled one of the furs up beneath her arms to cover her nakedness. "Why, Rhys? Why shouldn't you have? We've always had feelings for each other. Feelings that wouldn't have changed if things had happened differently."

He cursed under his breath again, then turned and pulled on his still-damp breeches. "But things didn't happen differently."

"That's not our fault. You know as well as I do that we

have strong feelings for each other. We've had those feelings for well over a year."

"You hated me for months," he pointed out.

She rubbed a hand against her forehead. "Because I didn't know the truth. But I always wanted you, and you always wanted me."

Rhys scrubbed a hand through his hair. He was bloody well tempted to tell her why he hadn't made love to her. But what good could possibly come from it? "Damn it, Julianna. That doesn't change the facts now. You're betrothed. That means something."

Anger flashed in her eyes. "Did it mean something when you were kissing me at the tree line? Did it mean something when you were touching me with your *tongue* just now?"

"Yes, damn it. We had a momentary lapse of judgment," he ground out.

"Both times?" she countered.

"Both times," he echoed, his voice flat.

The look in her eyes was a mixture of anger and recrimination. "No, Rhys. You're using that as an excuse. You know as well as I do what we have, what we've meant to each other."

He clenched his jaw. "Please, Julianna. For once in my blasted life, I'm trying to do the right thing. You're betrothed to Murdock."

"I don't love him."

"Don't say that."

She tossed a hand in the air. "We both know it's true." Tears filled her eyes and ran down her cheeks. She stared at him helplessly. "Do you love *me*, Rhys?" she asked, her gaze fiercely locked with his.

They stayed that way for what felt like endless seconds, neither of them saying a word.

Her jaw clenched, she pulled her shift on first, then her

habit. She stood and straightened her skirts. "Never mind. I should get back to the manor house. For Mama's sake."

CHAPTER TWENTY-SEVEN

J ulianna made the last several hundred yards of the trip back to the stables alone. Rhys had waited in the copse of trees watching her, in case her mother was still in the stables. He didn't want to risk the duchess seeing him and asking a lot of questions.

He needn't have worried. When Julianna rode Alabaster back into the stables, a large group gathered to welcome her, but her mother was not there. The stablemaster quickly informed her that they'd convinced Mama to return to her bedchamber and wait for word.

First, Mr. Hereford hurriedly dispatched Henry to the manor house to inform the duchess that her daughter had returned, then the stablemaster helped Julianna down from the horse and quickly wrapped a blanket around her shoulders.

"Are you all right?" Lord Clayton asked. He'd obviously been out in the rain too because he was soaking wet along with half the stablehands.

"I'm sorry to have worried all of you," Julianna said to the assembled group, wrapping the blanket more tightly over her shoulders. Guilt swamped her. "I'm sorry to have put you all to such trouble," she added.

Julianna was carted back to the house posthaste by a pair of groomsmen who turned her over to a pair of housemaids inside the house. From there, the maids escorted her back up to her bedchamber where her hovering mother insisted that she lie down and rest to prevent herself from catching a cold.

"Where were you, Julianna?" Mama asked after Julianna was safely dressed in her nightrail and snuggled under the covers in her bed.

Mary sat by her bedside, silently holding her hand.

"I took one of the Arabians out for a ride," Julianna explained.

"In the middle of a storm?" Mama shook her head, the worried expression still on her face.

"It wasn't storming when I left, but I am terribly sorry I worried you, Mama," Julianna replied.

Her mother didn't ask why she hadn't been wet when she returned, and Julianna had no intention of telling either her mother or her dear younger sister the details. No. She'd already decided on the long, silent ride back to the stables. Her afternoon with Rhys and what had transpired between them would go with her to her grave.

Today, she *finally* realized she had no future with Rhys. He'd made it clear that he would not be a party to her breaking things off with Murdock. And if Rhys didn't love her enough to stand up on a proverbial sideboard for her, did she even *want* to spend the rest of her life with him?

She'd been tempted, so blessed tempted, to blurt out that she loved him. She knew she loved him. Knew it deep down, but she refused to be the one to lay her heart on a chopping block again. What if she'd told him and he'd still refused her? She couldn't live with that the rest of her days. Another mistake with Rhys might prove fatal to her heart.

Besides, if he couldn't say it, neither would she. Those moments they'd stared into each other's eyes, both searching for the truth. If he truly loved her, he would have been able to admit it. Like Lord Kendall did with Frances Wharton. And Rhys hadn't.

In addition to his other sins, Rhys clearly didn't even love her enough to face damage to his or her reputation, regardless of how insignificant it might be. Lord knew the *ton* would be talking about Kendall and Miss Wharton's scandal far longer than if she cried off from Murdock to marry a man she'd courted before.

But Julianna knew now that her engagement to Murdock was merely an excuse Rhys was using, because once again, he didn't want to tell her the truth. And the truth was that he didn't actually love her.

She'd made a mistake involving herself with him again during the house party. She'd told herself that she'd only done it in order to get him to lose his bet. But now she realized that all she'd done was play with fire and burn herself. She didn't give a care about the bet any longer. It didn't matter if he won or lost. All she cared about was getting away from here, away from him, and protecting her heart once more.

"I want you to rest now, dear," Mama said, interrupting Julianna's thoughts. "Get some sleep. Don't worry about dinner tonight. We'll have it brought up again. Lord Murdock has been asking after you. I'll send word that you're safe."

Julianna weakly nodded. The mention of Lord Murdock reminded her of something else she needed to say. "Mama," she called. "I want to leave tomorrow. To go back to London, if you and Mary have no objections." There were five more days left to the house party, but Julianna couldn't stay.

Mary gave her a sympathetic look and nodded.

"It's probably for the best, dear," Mama replied, also nodding. "You'll want to rest more, and home may be the best place to do it. Your father will be happy to see you."

Her mother was about to step out the door when Julianna called out to her again, "Mama?"

Her mother paused in the doorway. "Yes, dear?"

"Lord Murdock told me he wants to move up the wedding date. He's written to Papa. When Papa receives the letter, you may tell him it's fine with me."

Mary's gaze snapped to her face, her eyes wide with confusion and concern. Julianna gave her sister an encouraging nod.

"I don't see how we'll be able to plan such a large wedding any sooner, dear," Mama replied, sighing, "but I'll speak to your father about it."

"Thank you, Mama. We can always make it smaller."

Her mother left then, and Julianna sat in silence holding Mary's hand. What did it matter whether the wedding was next month or next year? Julianna was selling herself to the highest bidder. Love had no part of it. She might as well get it over with.

CHAPTER TWENTY-EIGHT

The next morning, Rhys helped the other stablehands put her coach to, but he couldn't bring himself to watch Julianna go. At least not from the front of the stables like the rest of the chaps. Instead, he was in the barn, watching silently from a window as the footmen loaded her trunks and helped her up into the carriage. She was going back to London escorted by her own coachman, footmen, and lady's maid. Apparently, her mother and Mary were staying till the end of the house party.

Rhys watched the coach pull away and turn down the gravel path toward the road leading out of the estate. Letting her go yesterday had been the hardest thing he'd ever had to do. It had physically hurt. But for perhaps the first time in his life, he'd done the right thing. The noble thing. The selfless thing. Oh, he'd thought he was doing the right thing when he'd written her that blasted letter. But this was something different altogether. He would not have another chance. She was leaving his life forever.

Rhys swallowed hard. Julianna was no longer his. She hadn't been for months, and it was his fault. He'd been the one who had pushed her away. He'd been the one who had assumed the worst of her. And he'd be the one to suffer the consequences. A life without her.

She'd asked him if he loved her. He didn't think he knew what love meant. But if this aching pit in his belly—this feeling as if all of the happiness and joy had been sucked out of his life—meant that he loved her, then he did. He'd been a coward. He hadn't been able to tell her. It wasn't his right. After the mistakes he'd made, he had no business ruining her engagement by declaring his love. Her father already detested him. She told him herself that Montlake wouldn't allow her to cry off, and even if she tried, Rhys couldn't imagine Montlake suddenly consenting to *their* marriage.

No. It was better for Julianna this way even though the words *I love you* had been on the tip of Rhys's tongue. He'd *wanted* to say them, he truly had, but how could he? How could he tell her he loved her, knowing she'd still have to marry Murdock? Nothing could be more selfish.

Rhys watched until her coach disappeared into the distance. Then he leaned his head against the window frame and uttered a curse so loud it shook the beam above his head.

"You found her, didn't you?"

Rhys turned at the sound of Clayton's measured voice. "What?"

"You were the one who brought Lady Julianna back after the storm," Clayton continued.

Rhys lowered his head and scratched at the back of his neck. "How did you know?"

Clayton shrugged. "It was a simple process of elimination. Everyone else had returned with no luck. I couldn't find you."

"I took Midnight," Rhys admitted.

"I suspected as much. Where did you find her, at any rate?"

Rhys pressed a fist to his forehead. His head had been throbbing all morning. "The gamekeeper's cottage."

Clayton nodded. "Ah, the one place none of the rest of us bothered to look."

Rhys put his hands on his hips. "I'd shown it to her and her friends on their tour."

Clayton lifted both brows. "Tour? Friends?"

"Yes, Julianna had been coming out here quite a bit. To…" How could he possibly explain what she'd been doing? "Rile me."

Clayton left one brow arched. "To *rile* you? Or to visit you?"

"Visit me?" Rhys frowned. "Not at all. She'd been trying to get me to quit, to forfeit the bet."

"And…" Clayton replied quietly, "did she succeed?"

Rhys pulled himself away from the window and strode toward his friend. "You know, I believe she did. As of this moment, I'm officially resigning my position as a groomsman. Bell wins the bet."

Rhys clapped his friend on the back and continued walking toward the staircase. He intended to empty his berth and leave this blasted house party once and for all.

CHAPTER TWENTY-NINE

He should have known that Bell would appear. No doubt Clayton had rushed back to the manor house to find him. The marquess was standing next to Rhys's berth, leaning his shoulder against the wall, his arms folded negligently across his chest, when Rhys finally looked up and noticed him.

Damn, spies were bloody silent.

Rhys had been tossing his few belongings into the bag he'd brought with him. *Blast.* He would have to borrow one of Clayton's carriages to get back to London. His own wasn't due to arrive for him until after the house party ended.

In the meantime, he staunchly ignored the spy standing only a few paces away.

"You're forfeiting?" Bell finally drawled.

"That's right," Rhys said, kicking the ungodly mattress that he would *not* miss.

Bell contemplated his fingernails. "Care to explain why?"

"No, actually, I don't." Rhys gave his friend a tight smile and immediately changed the subject. "How's the hunt for the traitor going?"

Bell shrugged. "There've been some…complications."

Rhys arched a brow. "Complications?"

"Nothing I can't handle," Bell assured him.

"Of course," Rhys replied, "because you can handle anything, can't you, Lord Bellingham?"

Bell pushed himself off the wall and took a step forward. "You'll forgive me for asking why you're quitting. But I'm concerned. I happen to know how much you hate to lose bets."

"I don't give a bloody damn about this bet any longer." Rhys's voice was flat and emotionless.

"Don't you? Why, what in the world could make you stop caring about a bet that only a few days ago, you were intent upon winning?"

Rhys stuffed the last of his belongings into the bag. He turned his head to glare at Bell. "Do you have a point?"

Bell nodded sagely. "I always have a point."

Rhys hoisted the full bag to his shoulder. "Then please make it, because I'm leaving." He made to step past Bell. "Don't worry. I'll find a way to get you your money."

"Spare me," Bell replied. "I happen to be one of the few people who knows that you don't actually need the money from this bet. Or any other bet for that matter."

Rhys froze. He slowly turned to face Bell. "How in the bloody hell do you know that?"

Bell momentarily lifted his eyes skyward and sighed. "Why is everyone always forgetting that I'm a *spy*? Especially my friends."

Rhys couldn't help the smile that popped to his lips. "Fine. I'll have the money to you as soon as I get back to London. Is that what you want to hear?"

"No, actually, it's not. Because I don't give a bloody damn about the money either, and you know it. This has nothing to do with money."

"What do you want then?" Rhys shot back.

"I want to know what happened...between you and Lady Julianna. That is why you're forfeiting, isn't it?"

Rhys clenched his jaw. "Then you're going to be disappointed, I'm afraid, because I've no intention of telling you."

Bell stepped to the small window above the berth and glanced out at the paddock before turning to stare at Rhys again. "You're forgetting that I also happen to know why you agreed to go to France."

Rhys cursed under his breath again and he slowly folded his arms over his chest. "Oh, really? Do tell. I know you won't be satisfied until you've delivered your little speech. Go ahead."

Bell shrugged one shoulder. "You went to France to run away from the first lady you ever truly loved."

Rhys's nostrils flared and he narrowed his eyes to slits on the marquess. "Oh, is that why?" He did his best to sound nonchalant.

"Yes, actually." Bell nodded. "It's precisely why. Well, that and the fact that, despite your insistence upon letting everyone in the *ton* believe you're a drunken, penniless lout, you're really a good man who wanted to help his country."

"Please tell me more," Rhys drawled, sarcasm dripping from his tone. "I'm fascinated to hear what *I* think."

Bell leaned a hip against the windowsill. "Very well. I also happen to know that you love to go about pretending you're devil-may-care, but the truth is you're really worried that no one will truly love you for yourself, which is why you had to get away from Lady Julianna so quickly. She did love you for yourself. So, you invented a lot of excuses until you were finally able to hang it on that nonsense the *Times* printed, and that kept you conveniently mired in your bachelorhood."

Rhys clenched his fist. He wanted to punch the bastard in

the face so much his fingers ached. "Oh, so going *blind* is an excuse now? I see."

"Am I making you angry?" Bell continued in his own nonchalant tone. He moved from the window to stand on the opposite side of the mattress, blocking Rhys's path out of the berth.

"If you don't step out of my way, I *will* hit you," Rhys growled.

"Excellent," Bell drawled. "That tells me that I'm not missing my mark."

"I'm warning you, Bell—" Rhys ground out through clenched teeth.

"No, I'm warning *you*, Worth," the marquess shot back, his sky-blue eyes darkening.

"What?" Rhys tossed a hand in the air. "What are you warning me about?"

"If you let her go, you'll regret it for the rest of your life," Bell said quietly.

Rhys brushed past him, hitting Bell's shoulder, and knocking the marquess out of the way. "She's already gone."

CHAPTER THIRTY

***The Duke of Worthington's London Town House, Mid-
September 1814***

"**Y**our Grace," Rhys's butler, Lawson, intoned as he presented Rhys with a silver salver upon which sat the day's mail. Rhys absently pulled the letters from the tray and excused the man.

He tossed aside two bills and several invitations to parties and balls. The final piece of mail made him freeze. It was addressed from the Duke of Montlake.

Swallowing hard, Rhys yanked open the missive and unfolded it. His eyes scanned the page.

It, too, was an invitation. An invitation to the wedding of Lady Julianna Montgomery to the Marquess of Murdock. No doubt Montlake had had a smile on his face when he addressed *this* particular letter.

The invitation fell from Rhys's numb fingers onto the desktop. He took a deep breath. She was getting married. Early. Next month, in fact. Seems whatever important letter she'd written during the house party hadn't been about the wedding being moved up as he had guessed.

There hadn't been a day that had gone by since Rhys had returned from Clayton's estate that Bell's words hadn't haunted him. *If you let her go, you'll regret it for the rest of your life.* The bastard was right of course, but it didn't change the fact that Rhys was doing the selfless thing.

But Bell's other words were the ones that tore at him each night. Made him completely unable to sleep. Sometimes even unable to breathe. *You went to France to run away from the first lady you ever truly loved. She did love you for yourself. So, you invented a lot of excuses until you were finally able to hang it on that nonsense the* Times *printed, and that kept you conveniently mired in your bachelorhood.*

The only thing that made *those* blasted words fade temporarily into the background was the copious amounts of brandy Rhys had been drinking since his return. And even then, the words haunted him, streaming through his mind when he least wanted them.

As he stared down at the invitation that sat like an unwelcome bug on his desk, a hundred other thoughts raced across his brain. But in the end, he settled on the thought that he had wanted this. Pushed her to it, even. So be it.

But he *didn't* have to like it.

"Lawson!" he yelled at the top of his lungs.

Seconds later, the butler reappeared at the study door. "Your Grace?"

Rhys paced behind the desk, pushing back his hair and scratching his forehead. "Get me some brandy."

Lawson bowed. "As you wish, Your Grace. A glass of brandy."

"Not a glass, Lawson. The bottle."

CHAPTER THIRTY-ONE

"These will be lovely, don't you think, dear?"

"Yes, Mama, whatever you say." Julianna had been sitting in one of her father's drawing rooms staring at flowers all morning and she still couldn't bring herself to care. She didn't give a hairpin whether they had roses or lilies at the wedding. Lilacs were out of the question. It was too late in the year.

She took a deep breath and fought back the overwhelming anger and frustration she felt lately whenever she thought about the wedding, the marriage, or the rest of her life. She'd no idea why she couldn't just accept it all. She'd been raised for this. She'd been told her entire life that when it came time, she would make the most advantageous match with the most eligible gentleman and marry. She would be a wife, a mother, and a peeress. That's what had been planned for her since the cradle. So why was she so unhappy now that it was coming true?

She'd told herself a thousand times that she should call off the wedding. But she hadn't called it off. *Why* hadn't she called it off?

Because she was as stubborn as an ox, that's why. She'd wanted to throw the gauntlet at Rhys's feet. She knew he loved her. She knew he wanted her. She knew he *didn't* want her to marry Murdock, but he refused to tell the truth and save them both. Well, she refused too. If he was going to act as if the future and what happened to them didn't matter, then so would she.

Besides, what possible excuse could she give her parents for crying off? *I'm sorry; I won't marry the Marquess of Murdock because the Duke of Worthington loves me—even though he refuses to marry me.* It sounded ludicrous. And to make it worse, from time to time she continued to have the awful thought that perhaps Rhys had only been using her engagement to Murdock as an excuse not to marry her himself.

Well, if that's what he wanted, he was about to get it. This is what she'd been raised for all these years, wasn't it? To marry not for love but for title. The Duke of Worthington didn't want her, so she would marry the next most eligible bachelor. Just like the blessed *Times* had reported.

Julianna clenched her jaw and tossed down the fistful of flowers she'd been pretending to examine. She would cry if she had anymore tears left. She'd promised herself that she'd shed her last tear over Rhys Sheffield. He'd broken her heart —not once, but twice now—and bless it, she refused to allow him a third chance. No, she was going through with this wedding, and Rhys could go straight to hell.

Stratham, the butler, entered the room drawing room. "Miss Frances Wharton here to see Lady Julianna," he intoned.

Julianna glanced up, frowning. "Miss Wharton? For me? Not Lady Mary?"

Stratham cleared his throat. "She asked for you, my lady."

Julianna stood. Whatever Miss Wharton wanted to say to her, Julianna had a feeling it would best be said in private.

"Thank you, Stratham. Please show Miss Wharton into the white drawing room. I'll just pop over."

Without nothing more than a wave to her mother, who still sat amid the bouquets of flowers, Julianna slipped out of the door and made her way quickly across the hallway to the white drawing room. She settled herself on the chaise near the windows and rang for tea.

Seconds later, Miss Wharton entered the room, a tentative smile on her face.

"Good afternoon, Miss Wharton," Julianna said, standing and smiling at the shorter young woman.

"Oh, I'm so pleased to see you, Lady Julianna," Miss Wharton said. "Thank you for taking my call."

"Of course," Julianna replied, gesturing to the spot next to her on the chaise. "What did you want to speak to me about?"

Miss Wharton settled herself onto the seat before turning toward Julianna. "It may not be my place to say anything, Lady Julianna. And I do hope you'll send me on my way if this news is unwelcome to you, but...I thought perhaps you should know that you and I have a mutual acquaintance who is quite distraught at the prospect of your upcoming marriage."

Julianna arched a brow. Suspicion made her cross her arms over her chest. "Is our mutual acquaintance a duke, perhaps, Miss Wharton?"

Frances nodded. "He is."

Julianna narrowed her eyes on the younger woman. "He didn't ask you to come here, did he?"

Frances shook her head so resolutely one of her brown curls popped loose from her chignon and fell along her cheek. "No. Not at all. In fact, the truth is that if he or my intended, Lord Kendall, were to find out that I was here, I doubt either of them would be pleased."

"Oh, Miss Wharton. Please forgive my rudeness. Best

wishes on your upcoming nuptials. I'd read in the paper that you and Lord Kendall are to be married."

"Thank you, Lady Julianna. And if you are rude then I am doubly so, for not only did I fail to wish you the best on your impending marriage, but I fear I may be bringing news designed to...if not stop the wedding, then stall it, perhaps." Frances winced.

Julianna took a deep breath and folded her hands together in her lap. "Thank you for your concern, Miss Wharton. But without revealing personal details that I'd rather keep to myself, suffice it to say that the duke of our mutual acquaintance has made it quite clear that he is not interested in meddling in my affairs, specifically my upcoming wedding."

Frances frowned and looked down at the carpet. "Oh... how can that be?"

Julianna tilted her head to the side and studied Miss Wharton. "What do you mean?"

"My apologies, Lady Julianna," Frances replied, meeting Julianna's gaze again. "You must think I'm the veriest scatter-brain, given my inept attempts at delivering this message properly. I've always admired you for your properness, your beauty, your family connections, and your manners. And here I am blurting out things you may not want to hear."

Julianna sighed and looked away. "On the contrary, Miss Wharton. I've found more than one occasion to envy you of late. Most recently when your betrothed found it incumbent upon himself to stand atop a sideboard in front of Lord Clayton's entire guest list and declare his love for you."

Frances gave Julianna a sympathetic smile and reached over and patted her hand. "I can assure you, Lady Julianna, that what at the time seemed like a romantic gesture was anything but welcome to me that evening."

"Are you quite serious?" Julianna blinked at her. She

pressed her hand over her heart. "I thought what Lord Kendall did that night was the most romantic thing I'd ever witnessed."

Frances nodded slowly. "I suppose we both have secrets we'd like to keep, but please believe me when I tell you that our mutual acquaintance, ahem, the duke, forfeited the bet after you left."

Julianna's eyes went wide. "Are you quite certain?"

"Oh, yes," Miss Wharton continued. "Entirely certain. And I probably don't have to tell you it was for an ungodly sum of money." Frances lowered her voice. "One thousand pounds."

Julianna gulped. Good heavens. She'd never guessed it had been for *that* much. And Rhys had forfeited? Not lost because someone recognized him? That certainly told her something. If he'd lost that much, he might well be too deeply in debt to ever recover. A twinge of guilt tugged at her conscience.

"Furthermore," Miss Wharton continued, "this particular duke has been drinking constantly since he received the invitation to your wedding, and he cannot stop talking about you."

Julianna swallowed and glanced away. Frances was correct. She did not want to hear that. Drinking and talking didn't change anything.

"Miss Wharton," she replied. "I suppose we shall have to agree to disagree when it comes to what is important for a gentleman to do to demonstrate his love. For I envy you a man who would stand up on a sideboard for you. You said you admired me, but I'd trade anything I have for a man who loved me that much."

CHAPTER THIRTY-TWO

I t turned out that brandy didn't make anything better. It didn't give him clarity. It didn't help him to decide anything. It didn't even make him feel better, save for the few hours he managed to remain drunk as a wheelbarrow each evening. Which is why late one night, nearly a month after Rhys had received the invitation to Julianna's wedding in the post, he decided to take his bottle of brandy and go over to Kendall's house.

Not an hour later, his coach pulled up in front of the four-story town house in Belgravia and Kendall's butler soon showed Rhys into his friend's study.

Rhys stumbled over to one of the large leather chairs that sat in front of his friend's desk and laid his head on his hands, which he'd placed atop the imposing piece of furniture. He was attempting to stop his head from spinning. With little luck.

Minutes later, Kendall came stomping into the room.

"Must you be so loud?" Rhys grumbled, grabbing his head with both hands.

"My apologies," Kendall replied with a grin. "I thought I

was in my own house and *you'd* come to visit. Why are you here so late, by the by?"

Rhys forced himself to sit up and glared at his friend. "I seem to recall that after Lady Emily tossed you over, you spent five sodden days in a row at my house, drinking away your sorrows and ruing the day you met her."

"True, but am I missing something? Have you been tossed over?" Kendall asked, blinking at Rhys innocently.

"No," a thunderous scowl sat on Rhys's face, "but your involvement with Lady Emily is why I am so bloody well against ladies tossing over one man for another with a better title."

"You're making no sense, Worth, perhaps you should start over," Kendall said with a patient smile.

"Being noble and selfless is a lot of shite." Rhys pointed a finger in the air.

"*You've* been noble and selfless?" Skepticism dripped from Kendall's tone.

"I most certainly have," Rhys declared, pounding the desktop with his closed fist. "I let her go. I did the honorable thing."

Kendall took a deep breath. "I can only assume this is about Lady Julianna, correct?"

"Correct," Rhys replied, looking around the room as if searching for something. "Do you have any more brandy? I seem to have finished mine." He held his empty bottle upside down and stared at it as if he didn't understand what it was.

"Yes, I do, but no, you may not have any. You smell as if you've had far too much of it already."

Rhys narrowed his eyes on the earl. "Don't make me call you out, Kendall."

"Oh, dear, not drunken threats. This is bad." Kendall sighed again. "Very well, Bell was there to help me when I was a drunken fool in love who needed to hear a few choice words. I suppose the least I can do now is pass on the favor."

Rhys wrinkled his brow. "What are you talking about?" He righted the empty brandy bottle and thumped it atop the desk.

"Sit back," Kendall ordered. "Let me explain a few things to you."

"I don't want to hear anything Bell has to say," Rhys insisted. "He doesn't know what he's talking about."

"He *always* knows what he is talking about unfortunately, but don't worry. Bell told me he's already tried to explain the situation to you. Now, I fear it's my turn."

Letting go of the empty bottle, Rhys sat up straight and readjusted himself in the chair so that he was no longer slouching. "Explain what?"

Kendall tapped a finger along his cheek. "First of all, you're thinking of this entire thing all wrong."

Rhys blinked at him through blurry eyes. "Wrong?" he echoed. "What do you mean?"

"Was I upset when Lady Emily left me? Yes, but in retro-spect, she did me the biggest act of kindness of my life."

Rhys shook his head and narrowed his eyes on his friend. Kendall wasn't making any sense tonight. "What the devil are you talking about, man? She humiliated you. You were devastated."

"You're right, but it doesn't change the fact that if Lady Emily hadn't done what she did, I wouldn't have Frances now. I'm much happier with Frances than I ever could have been with Emily."

Rhys leaned back and rubbed both of his temples. The room was spinning, and nothing made sense any longer. "She did you an act of kindness?"

"A considerable act of kindness. If I run across her one day, I intend to thank her, actually. Don't you see, Worth? If she had married me without loving me, she would have done me the greatest disservice of all. I'd have been stuck with her for life. Frances loves me for who I am. That's the greatest gift and well worth the temporary humility I felt about Emily tossing me over."

Rhys shook his head, trying to ensure he interpreted his friend's words correctly. "So, if Julianna tossed over Murdock, she might be doing him an act of kindness."

Kendall lifted both shoulders. "If she doesn't love him, she would be."

Rhys's heart thumped in his chest. Why had he never seen it this way before?

"What's more," Kendall continued.

Rhys sank back into his chair and stared at his friend. "There's more?"

"Yes, the difference between your situation and mine with Lady Emily is that you and Julianna had feelings for each other *before* she became engaged to Murdock. She actually cared for you before she met him, which means it's highly likely that *were* she to pick you, she would be choosing you for true love and not your title."

Rhys allowed the words he'd just heard to sink into his addled brain. It was true. He *had* known Julianna before she'd met the Marquess of Murdock. He *had* had feelings for her then, and she had had them for him. She'd said as much.

Rhys lurched to his feet and swiped his hair away from his forehead. "By God, man, I do believe I finally understand."

Kendall inclined his head toward Rhys. "Excellent. I'm thrilled to hear it, because you've been acting like a complete horse's arse for weeks."

Rhys lurched across the desk and grabbed Kendall by the cravat. "Good God. What day is it?"

Kendall pulled Rhys's hand away and gave him a skeptical look. "You truly don't know?"

"Is it the fifteenth? She's getting married the morning of the fifteenth." His throat was dry and true panic coursed through his veins.

"You're in luck," Kendall replied with a grin. "It's the fourteenth."

Rhys whirled around to stare at the clock on the mantelpiece. It was nearly midnight, which meant he only had a matter of hours to find her. Find her and somehow convince her to marry him. Because he may have made the biggest mistake of his life *twice* in the last eighteen months, but damned if he was going to make it a third time.

"I have to talk to her, Kendall. I must find her." Rhys turned and dashed toward the door.

"Do you really think it's best to go *now*? You're inebriated, old chap," Kendall said, following his friend down the corridor toward the front door.

"I've no time to waste." Rhys grabbed his coat, hat, and gloves from the shocked-looking butler and ripped open the front door. "Just point me in the direction of Montlake's town house."

Kendall rolled his eyes. "I'm entirely certain I'm going to regret telling you this, but now that I think of it, Frances did mention something about Lady Julianna wanting a man who'd jump on a sideboard in front of the Prince Regent for her."

Rhys turned to stare at him, his brow tightly furrowed. "What? What are you saying?"

Kendall sighed. "I'm saying you'll need to make a grand gesture if you're going to win her back, so I'll do better than pointing you in the right direction. I'll take you there myself."

He asked the butler to have his coach brought round and pulled on his own coat.

CHAPTER THIRTY-THREE

R hys nearly jumped from Kendall's coach before it came to a complete stop across from the Duke of Montlake's town house. He righted himself and then ran across the road and up the steps of the imposing structure.

Kendall followed close behind, obviously keeping an eye on his drunken friend.

Rhys rapped on the door loud and long until an equally imposing butler answered the summons.

"May I help you?" The butler obviously remembered Rhys from his prior visits to Julianna because his demeanor changed the moment he saw Rhys. "Your Grace," he intoned, bowing.

"I must speak to Lady Julianna, immediately," Rhys replied.

The butler turned ashen white. "His Grace has asked that Lady Julianna not be disturbed tonight," the man said, clearly referring to Julianna's father. "It is the eve of her..." the butler cleared his throat uncomfortably, "wedding."

Rhys grabbed the butler's shoulders and stared him in the

eye. "I bloody well know that, man, that's why I need to speak to her."

Kendall pulled Rhys away from the poor butler, who couldn't have looked more astonished if he'd just been assaulted by the queen.

"Apologies, kind sir," Kendall said before Rhys could open his mouth again. He pushed Rhys behind him. "But we have reason to believe Lady Julianna would like to hear what Lord Worthington has to say. Could you please allow us in, and go fetch her?"

The butler glanced about uncomfortably. "Come into the drawing room. I can only agree to ask His Grace for permission." The butler clearly didn't want any more of a spectacle to unfold on the front steps of his master's house.

"But I need to speak to Julianna," Rhys moaned.

Kendall turned and whispered in his ear, "Patience, my friend. At least we're making it past the front door."

The butler showed them into a white drawing room and shut the door.

"Do you know where Julianna's rooms are?" Kendall asked Rhys the moment the butler left.

"No. I don't," Rhys said, pacing anxiously back in forth in front of the windows, feeling like a caged animal.

Kendall bit the inside of his cheek. "Well, I suggest you take your best attempt at guessing, because I have every reason to believe Montlake will not let you past this drawing room."

"He's never been my biggest proponent," Rhys admitted with a wry smile.

Kendall opened the door and peered out into the corridor. "The foyer is empty. I suggest you make a break for the staircase and hope to hell you choose the correct bedchamber."

CHAPTER THIRTY-FOUR

R hys was only halfway up the staircase when a commotion in the foyer made him glance down. Montlake was there, along with his butler, who'd just caught sight of Rhys. When the butler pointed up at him, Rhys sprinted for the top of the staircase and flew down the second-floor corridor that was lined with doors on either side.

Footsteps thundering on the staircase told him he didn't have much time. He opened the first door on the right. "Julianna?"

"Who is it?" came Mary Montgomery's sleepy voice.

Blast. He'd chosen poorly. "My apologies," he said softly before backing out and pulling the door shut. He'd turned to try the next door when the Duke of Montlake lunged at Rhys and tackled him to the ground.

"Get out of my house, Worthington!" Montlake yelled as they wrestled together on the floor.

"I must speak to Julianna. I love her!" Rhys yelled.

"Not while I'm alive and breathing," Montlake thundered back.

"Why are you so against me?" Rhys asked, trying to push the much-heavier man off of him.

"You're a drunken lout," Montlake insisted. He had Rhys by the ankle.

"No, I'm not." Rhys tried to kick off his hold.

"Really? At present you appear to be drunken, and I can vouch for you being a lout," was Montlake's reply.

"I love your daughter," Rhys shot back.

"So do I, and I refuse to allow her reputation be sullied by your antics."

Rhys had nearly got his leg free when the door to the bedchamber he had entered opened and Lady Mary came out wearing a dressing gown.

She glanced down at the two men on the floor. "What is happening, Papa?" Her eyes were wide, and her voice was filled with concern.

"Go back to bed, darling," Montlake answered. "I'm just ridding the house of some vermin."

"Mr. Worthy?" Mary asked, squinting down at the two men who were still wrestling each other on the floor.

"Who?" Montlake asked.

"Why are you fighting Mr. Worthy, the groomsman from Lord Clayton's estate?"

They both stopped wrestling and stared up at Mary. Then they rolled apart and sat across from each other, their backs against the opposite walls, both still breathing heavily from their exertions, both still giving the other a distrustful stare.

"What are you talking about, Mary?" her father asked.

Mary leaned down as if to get a better view of Rhys in the dark. "Yes, that's him. That's Mr. Worthy from Lord Clayton's estate. Anna and I met him during our stay in August."

Rhys, who felt as if he'd sobered up almost entirely since he'd arrived at the Montlake residence, bowed his head and nodded at Mary. "Good to see you again, milady."

"Milady?" Montlake nearly shouted. He stared at Rhys as if he'd lost his mind.

"What are you doing here, Mr. Worthy? Oh, have you come to see Anna?" Mary asked, a sweet smile on her face.

"I have," Rhys replied, nodding vigorously. "I've come to see Anna. Will you please tell her I'm here?"

Mary swiveled around, obviously about to do just that, when her father's voice thundered, "You will do no such thing, Mary."

Mary froze. She turned again and stared at her father with wide eyes.

"I've no idea why you're calling him 'Mr. Worthy' or why he's calling you 'milady,'" Montlake continued, "but this ruffian is none other than the Duke of Worthington, and I refuse to allow him to see your sister."

Mary's eyes widened even further if that was possible. "The Duke of Worth—"

Rhys bit his lip and gave Mary his most apologetic smile. "I'm sorry, Lady Mary. It's quite a long story and I—"

"Have no time to tell it," Montlake finished for him.

The butler was standing at the top of the staircase watching the entire debacle unfold.

"Stratham, get two of the footmen and toss out this black-guard," Montlake ordered.

Apparently, two of the footmen had already been prepared for just such an order, as they appeared seconds later and wrestled Rhys to his feet.

The footmen wrenched Rhys toward the staircase and down the steps, where Kendall was waiting with their hats.

"I suppose we should go?" Kendall asked with a sardonic smile.

The butler threw open the front door and the footmen tossed Rhys unceremoniously down the front steps. Then they turned back to Kendall.

Kendall put up a palm. "I prefer to leave on my own, gentlemen," he replied, stepping through the doorway and hurrying down the steps to help up his friend.

Rhys allowed Kendall to give him a hand. He stood and examined himself. He had a bloody scrape on his arm and his ankle had been twisted in the fall. He tried to take a step forward and had to lean on Kendall for support.

The butler slammed the front door shut, and Rhys stood there glaring at the town house, his hands on his hips.

Blast. Blast. Blast.

Kendall pursed his lips. "Well, it certainly seems as if *that* didn't go as planned."

CHAPTER THIRTY-FIVE

Julianna stirred awake when the door to her bedchamber opened and then shut. The soft padding of feet and a candle flickering to light near her bed revealed her sister had entered the room. Was she imagining it, or had she heard a vague commotion in the hallway a few minutes ago?

"Anna," Mary called softly. "Anna, wake up."

Julianna pushed herself up against the pillows and rubbed her eyes. "What is it, Mary? Are you all right? What time is it?"

"I'm fine. I think it's nearly one o'clock." Mary took a seat on the foot of Julianna's bed. She held the candle holder in her hand. "I came to tell you something, Anna. Something important."

Julianna's heart beat faster. Had her sister come to tell her she should call off the wedding in the morning? "If you're here to talk about Lord Murdock, there's something I need to tell you first."

Mary nodded. "Go ahead."

Julianna took a deep breath. "I've decided to call off the wedding."

"What?" Mary's eyes went wide. "But the wedding is this morning."

Julianna nodded. "I know. I decided last night before I fell asleep. It's the first time in weeks that I've been able to fall asleep actually. That's how I know it's the right decision."

"What do you intend to do, Anna?" Mary asked her, searching her face.

"I plan to inform Lord Murdock at sun-up. I expect he'll take it well. When I asked him last week whether he loved me, he asked me what love had to do with marriage."

Mary scrunched up her nose. "That doesn't sound terribly romantic."

"I agree. And after I inform Lord Murdock that I am not marrying him, I plan to go find the Duke of Worthington and tell him I love him."

"You love Worthington?" Mary asked, a frown wrinkling her brow.

"Yes, and even if I tell him I love him and he doesn't say it back, I know I'll regret it forever if I don't at least try. I've spent my whole life living up to someone else's expectations of how I should behave. I deserve happiness. I deserve a chance at true love, and I think I can only have that with Worthington."

Mary's eyes filled with tears. "I'm so happy for you, Anna, and I truly think you're doing the right thing. I actually came in here to talk about Lord Worthington."

"You did?" Julianna replied, blinking at her sister through the darkness. "What about him?"

Mary winced. "Let me preface this by saying I probably should have told you this long before now."

Julianna's heart thumped so fast it hurt. "Tell me what?"

"Well, for one thing, I wasn't actually interested in riding lessons at Lord Clayton's house party."

Julianna shook her head. "Mary, you woke me up at one o'clock in the morning to tell me you didn't really want to take riding lessons at a house party we left over a month ago?"

This time Mary bit her lip. "Yes. I wasn't particularly interested in Lord Mixton, either."

Julianna shook her head. "I suppose that explains why he hasn't been around since." She rubbed a hand across her forehead. "Mary, dear, are you feeling all right?"

Mary took a deep breath. "I'm not doing a particularly good job at admitting to something, Anna, but the truth is that I always knew Mr. Worthy the groomsman was really the Duke of Worthington."

Julianna's head spun as if she'd been thrown from a horse. "What?" She'd heard each of her sister's words, but somehow, they didn't seem to make sense.

Mary nodded. "Yes, I knew it was him, and I invented excuses like going to look at flowers on the far side of the lake and needing to take riding lessons in order for you to have reasons to spend more time with him."

Julianna felt as if the wind had been knocked from her chest. "What? How did you know?"

Mary bit her lip. "While it's true that I never *formally* met the duke," she continued, "the truth is that little sisters tend to do things like sneak to the top of the staircase and peer into the foyer when older sisters' *beaux* come courting. I heard Stratham call him by name."

Julianna pressed her fingers to her temples. Wait? You saw Worthington from atop the staircase well over a year ago and you remembered him when he was pretending to be a groomsman at a house party?"

Mary shrugged and a coy smile popped to her lips. "He's

ever so handsome, Anna. Not exactly someone whose countenance one forgets."

Julianna's mouth formed a wide O. "If you knew, why did you never ask me why he was pretending to be a groomsman?"

Mary shrugged again. "You both obviously had your reasons for pretending. Far be it from me to ruin the charade. In fact, I continued to pretend even just now when Papa was fighting him in the corridor."

"What!" Julianna bolted upright.

Mary folded her hands together calmly. "Yes, well, that is more precisely the reason I've come. The Duke of Worthington just arrived to declare his love for you and Papa had him tossed out into the street."

CHAPTER THIRTY-SIX

"T here's no help for it," Kendall said, hoisting himself up into his carriage. "Perhaps you can write her a letter."

Rhys gave the earl a glowering stare. "You can't be serious?" Limping, he'd retreated across the road to Kendall's carriage, but he'd yet to climb inside. Instead, he was still staring up at Montlake's town house. "There has to be some way for me to scale the wall," he muttered.

"You *can't* be serious?" Kendall retorted.

"Aren't you the one who told me that Julianna wanted a man who'd climb onto a sideboard for her?"

"A sideboard, yes, a second-story window? That's risking death."

Rhys glowered again. "Are you saying you wouldn't try to scale the wall if Frances was up there and you had no other way of getting to her?"

Kendall cursed under his breath. "Damn it. You're right." He jumped back down to help Rhys contemplate the wall.

The two of them were staring at the sheer flatness of the

thing, their heads cocked in opposite directions, when a noise to their left caught their attention.

"Rhys," Julianna's voice rang out.

He swiveled around, at first doubting his sight. But Julianna was there. She had on a dressing gown and was wearing slippers. "What are you doing out here?" Rhys asked. "Did you hear us fighting in the corridor?"

"No." Julianna shook her head. "Mary woke me. She said I had a visitor and I'd better hurry because Papa had thrown him out."

Rhys threw back his head and laughed. "Remind me to buy Mary a hothouse full of buttercups."

Tears sparkled in Julianna's eyes. She took a step closer to him. "Why are you here, Rhys?"

Rhys limped over to her and took her hands in his, rubbing his thumbs across her knuckles. His gaze caught hers. "I may not have had the chance to climb up on a sideboard, but I came to tell you I love you, Julianna. I know I should have said it sooner, but I'm saying it now. And if you'll forgive me for being a damn fool not once but twice, I want to ask you to be my wife."

"Let me assure you, Lady Julianna, he was quite prepared to attempt to scale the wall," Kendall added, leaning from inside of the coach.

"You were going to climb up the wall?" Julianna asked, searching his face. "Up to my bedchamber?"

"That's right," Rhys replied. "I was just about to ask Kendall here if he happened to have a length of rope in his coach."

"The answer is no," Kendall chimed in.

Julianna squeezed Rhys's hands. "Oh, Rhys, even *contemplating* scaling a wall is better than jumping up on a sideboard as far as I'm concerned. And I heard you wrestled with Papa over me."

Rhys limped one step closer to her.

Julianna looked down at his foot, worry lining her countenance. "You're limping. Your injury from France?"

"Yes, that and the toss into the street, courtesy of two of your father's footmen. But I haven't slept in days. I couldn't stop thinking about you getting married to the wrong man." Rhys dropped to one knee. "Julianna, here, in front of your father's house, I am asking you to please become my wife."

Tears slid down Julianna's cheeks. "You do know my wedding is in a few hours?"

Rhys shook his head. "No, your wedding was *supposed* to be in a few hours. Now, I hope, it's cancelled."

"I'll have to toss over Murdock, you know?" She stared at him intently.

"I know. But Murdock will live, and according to my friend Kendall, here, he'll be better off for it."

"He will. He truly will," Kendall dutifully agreed, in a muffled voice from inside the coach.

Julianna pulled Rhys up, jumped into his arms, and hugged him. He lifted and spun her around in a somewhat lopsided circle and kissed her passionately.

"The truth is, I was going to call off the wedding this morning and come looking for you," Julianna said as he kissed her.

He lowered her back to the ground and grabbed her hands again. "You were?"

"Yes, we're both obviously too stubborn for our own good. We never should have let it go this long."

"Agreed," came Kendall's voice.

"I love you, Rhys. I love you and I should have told you as much that day at the gamekeeper's cottage."

Rhys pulled her into his arms and hugged her. "I should have told you then, too."

Inside the coach, Kendall cleared his throat. "May we go

home now? I hate to mention it, but it's quite late, and standing about in the street doesn't seem particularly prudent, even if we are in Mayfair."

Rhys and Julianna both laughed.

"Yes," Rhys replied, "but you'll have to drop us off at my town house, because I intend to thoroughly compromise Lady Julianna here so that her father has no choice but to approve of our marriage." He paused and looked at Julianna. "With your permission, of course, my lady."

"Permission enthusiastically granted, Your Grace," she replied with a laugh, sparing a blush for Kendall, before allowing Rhys to help her up into the coach.

They set off at a fast clip toward Rhys's nearby town house.

CHAPTER THIRTY-SEVEN

Minutes later, Kendall's coach pulled to a stop in front of Rhys's town house.

"I promise that if asked, I will insist that I know nothing about either of your whereabouts and that I have neither seen nor heard a thing tonight," Kendall announced with a resolute nod.

"Thank you," Rhys said to the earl, inclining his head as he helped Julianna alight from the coach.

"I will also neither confirm nor deny the rumor that is certain to begin that the Duke of Worthington tried to scale the wall of the Duke of Montlake's town house in order to declare his love for Lady Julianna," Kendall added.

Rhys frowned at his friend. "Why would you think such a rumor would start?"

"Because I intend to start it, of course," Kendall replied with a wink before pulling the door to the coach shut and ordering his coachman to drive home.

Moments later, with Julianna by his side, Rhys managed to sneak into his own house. They giggled like school children as they stole up the darkened staircase to his bedchamber, Rhys still limping all the way.

Inside the large room, candles were lit on the mantelpiece and either side of the bed. A sapphire blue bedspread covered the enormous bed. Two chairs and a small chaise sat in front of the fireplace, which took up an entire wall. The opposite wall was comprised of windows from floor to ceiling and large damask sapphire curtains had been drawn closed in front of them.

The door from the adjoining room that housed Rhys's wardrobe cracked open.

"I won't be needing your assistance tonight, Gilbert," Rhys called to his valet, a sly smile on his face.

The door shut again as quickly as it had opened.

"Don't you think you should allow him to look at your ankle?" Julianna asked with a laugh.

"Not tonight. He can look at my blasted ankle tomorrow." Rhys hopped over to her and pulled her into his arms. "Tonight is for us."

Julianna kissed him and then pulled away.

He frowned. "We don't have to do this, you know."

"Are you jesting?" she replied with another laugh. "I've been waiting for this for well over a year. Besides, something tells me Papa won't agree to our match if we don't give him something to...*ahem*...agree with."

Rhys scratched at the back of his neck. "Yes, well, I just hope he doesn't call me out."

Julianna shook her head. "He won't. He'll be angry at first, to be certain, but in the end, Mama will convince him it's for the best. Mama can always convince him."

"Will you always be able to convince me?" he asked, kissing the edge of her lips.

"I hope so," Julianna replied with a smile.

Rhys pulled her close and kissed her thoroughly. "I love you, Julianna. I cannot wait to marry you."

"I love you, too, Rhys," she said before turning quickly and pointing to her back. "Unbutton me."

Rhys chuckled. "You don't waste any time, do you?"

She laughed too. "You cannot blame me. I happen to have a bit of experience with you and I know how good it's going to be."

His grin was downright arrogant. "Well, in that case." His fingers worked at the back of her gown. As soon as it was unbuttoned, she turned back to face him and he helped her pull the gown completely over her head.

Rhys carefully made his way over to the tufted stool that ran the length of the end of the bed. He sat and shucked his boots.

Julianna joined him and helped him remove his coat, cravat, and shirt. Her hands splayed across his broad chest. "You don't know how tempting you were all those times I saw you in the stables without your shirt."

"And you don't know how tempting *you* were. Especially that day you rode astride." He shook his head.

"Really?" She blinked at him.

"Those breeches? Torture," he replied. "Absolute torture."

"Come to bed," Julianna said, a coquettish smile on her lips. She helped him around the edge of the bed, and he hoisted himself up on the mattress and watched as she pulled her night rail over her head and threw it to the end of the bed.

She stood in front of him, entirely, gloriously naked.

Rhys's gaze devoured her. "You're magnificent."

She glanced at him, tentatively biting her lip. "Your injury isn't going to keep you from–"

"Not a chance," he shot back, shaking his head vigorously.

She laughed and climbed up on the bed next to him. "I

suppose you'll need assistance removing your breeches, however."

His eyes sparkled. "Yes, my lady. I'm entirely at your mercy."

She pushed him back onto the pillows and he laid there with his hands beneath his head, while her fingers moved to the buttons of his breeches. She painstakingly popped each one open, one after the other, while Rhys struggled to keep his raging cockstand under control.

When the buttons were all undone, Julianna motioned for him to lift his hips, then she tugged on his breeches with both hands, pulling them down over his hips until they were inside out, and pulled them off over his ankles.

She tossed the garment to the floor and let her gaze travel over his long, lean body. "You're gorgeous, Rhys."

"I believe that's what I'm supposed to say to you." He sat up and pulled her toward him. Then, he slid down the mattress. She was on her knees in front of him and he lined his face up with her sex. He cupped his hands over her buttocks to keep her in place. Then he licked deep and long in between her folds.

Julianna's eyes went wide. "I didn't know we could…" Her voice trailed off in what sounded like embarrassment.

She was referring to their positions. "Oh, sweetheart, there are so many ways we can love each other. I can't wait to teach you each and every one of them."

She braced her hands on his shoulders, holding onto him while he continued to lick her again and again. Wet warmth pooled between her legs and when he let go of one of her hips, he trailed a finger down between her legs and slowly slid it inside of her.

"Rhys," she called, her knees a bit wobbly. She held on to his shoulders as he slid his finger in and out.

"Let me touch you, Julianna," he said between licks.

"Yes," she called, tossing her head back, her long blond hair trailing down to her buttocks.

Rhys continued to lick her again and again, while his finger kept up its gentle assault until he touched a spot inside her that made her cry out.

She stared down at him in wonder. "What was that?" she breathed.

"Shh," he whispered against her thigh. "Just let me touch you." He slid his finger in again, pressing against the tender spot once more. Julianna's knees buckled and he sucked her as she cried out and collapsed in a heap against him.

Then he turned her over and laid her against the pillows, his body trailing back down between her legs.

His mouth reached the apex between her thighs again.

Her body trembled, and her breathing came in short pants. "Rhys, I don't think I can—"

His mouth descended onto her again. "Yes," he breathed. "I promise you, you can." His grin was wicked.

He licked her again and again until her body began to thrum once more, and she fisted her hands in the sheets on either side of her hips.

His finger returned to slide inside of her and this time he angled it to press on the sensitive spot from another direction.

"Oh, God, Rhys," she called, her head thrown back, her breasts thrust forward, her gorgeous body writhing with pleasure.

He licked her again and sucked on her nub, pressing against the sensitive spot until she called out his name, tears rolling down her cheeks.

He pulled himself up to look at her. "Are you all right, Julianna?"

"I…" She was panting, unable to breathe. "I…think so. I didn't know that much pleasure was possible."

His smile was smug. He nuzzled at her neck. "I want it to be good for you, my darling. Always."

"It was good, Rhys," she said, wiping away the tears. "So good. I don't know why I'm crying."

"It's your body's natural reaction to the release, Love." He held her like that until her breathing returned to rights. She made a move to turn and descend down his body, but he held her against him.

"I want to please you, Rhys, the way you did me," she said, her brow furrowed in confusion.

"Tonight, Julianna, I don't think I could take it. I want to make love to you." He kissed her deeply. "Let me make love to you."

She smiled at him and nodded. "By all means."

Rhys settled her back against the pillows again and moved atop her, his body trembling.

"You're shaking," she murmured, wrapping her arms around his neck.

"I'm nervous," he admitted humbly. "I've never done this out of love before."

Julianna's heart nearly exploded. For a proud man like Rhys to admit something like that to her meant more than anything else. She cupped his face in her hands. She might be a virgin, but he was too in a way. "I love you, Rhys. Make me yours."

His cock probed between her legs and Rhys held his breath as he slid into Julianna's wet warmth. Nothing in his entire life had prepared him for the riot of emotions he felt as he finally joined his body with hers. Sex had always just been a physical act before. Now that he was doing it out of love, it was so much more.

He slid all the way in to the hilt and opened his eyes to search her face. "Did I hurt you, Julianna?"

"Not at all," she assured him, a wide smile on her face.

He leaned down and kissed her with all the love and lust he felt for her. Then, he began to move.

He stroked slowly at first, allowing her body time to adjust to him. As sweat glistened on their skin, he began to stroke longer, deeper. He clenched his teeth, bracing himself against the ungodly pleasure, wanting to prolong it for her, to ensure she felt good yet again.

"Wrap your legs around me, Julianna," he commanded.

She did so without hesitating and in that moment, one of his most erotic fantasies came true: Julianna's perfect long legs were wrapped around him as he rode her. Her head tossed back and forth on the pillow, a look of pure pleasure on her face.

It was too much. His legs tensed. His thighs ached. He wanted to come so badly he hurt with the need. He moved his hand down between them, to stroke his thumb against her, intent on making her come once more.

"Rhys," she said. "I want your pleasure."

She'd said it in such a commanding voice, he had no choice but to obey the lady. Pulling her tight against him, he pumped into her again and again before releasing his seed in the most mind-numbing orgasm of his entire life. Then he collapsed atop her, his heart pounding, his body trembling, more satisfied than he'd ever been.

Moments passed before his breathing righted and Rhys rolled to his side, immediately pulling Julianna against him and wrapping his arms around her. "You're mine," he breathed. "And I'm yours."

"Forever," she replied, kissing his forearm.

They laid like that for several minutes, both basking in the glow of their lovemaking before Julianna finally pulled out of his arms and pushed herself up against the pillows next to him.

Her face turned serious. "I want you to know something, Rhys."

"What's that, Love?" He trailed his hand along her outer thigh.

"I know you lost the bet and I don't care if you're poor. In fact, you may use my dowry to pay off your debts if you like."

Rhys gently reached up and stroked her cheek with his fingers. "Thank you, my love, but the truth is that I am not in debt."

Her brow furrowed. "You're not?"

He shook his head. "Not a farthing. In fact, I've managed to double the amount my father left several times over."

Her mouth fell open. "How is that possible? The papers are always reporting how much you lose at Hollister's, and Lady Helen said—"

A wicked grin spread across his lips. He pulled her fingers up to his mouth and kissed them. "Haven't we learned that the papers aren't always right? And something tells me Lady Helen doesn't know much about my financial situation." He rolled his eyes comically.

"You *haven't* lost your fortune?" she asked, still agog.

"Afraid not. You see, after I lose for the sake of the papers —to keep the gossip mills happy—I go elsewhere and win exorbitant sums."

Julianna shook her head again. "Why would you do that? Why would you want everyone to think you lost?"

Rhys let out a long, loud sigh. "For the same reason I didn't want to believe that you truly cared about me." He pushed himself up against the headboard, propping a pillow behind him. "I've spent my life being convinced—mainly by my father —that women would only want me for my money and title."

"And when you saw the story in the paper, you decided I was one of them," she murmured.

He kissed her fingers again. "I think I'd convicted you in my head long before that, Julianna. But it was my own insecurity that I was trying to hide from. I should have told you the truth from the beginning. I was far too arrogant, or at least I pretended to be, but mostly that was just what I want people to think about me. I finally had to face the fact that I'm not always right. Being a servant was humbling. It taught me many things, I'm thankful to say. I can honestly say that I won't pretend to be something I'm not anymore. Even a drunken, penniless, lout."

"Or a groomsman?" She smiled at him.

"Or a groomsman," he replied with a laugh.

She threaded her fingers through his. "I was wrong too, Rhys. I should have told you I loved you. Instead, I allowed my anger with you for believing the worst about me and my own pride stand in the way of our happiness. I was far too stubborn for my own good."

Rhys brought their hands to his lips and kissed her wrist. "Lord help our future children, Love. They will no doubt be doubly stubborn."

"I'm already worried about their marriage prospects," she said with a laugh.

"Speaking of marriage, I'll go speak to your father first thing in the morning," Rhys said with a resolute nod.

Julianna traced her fingertip along the edge of the sheet. She nodded. "Yes, and while you're doing that, I must find Lord Murdock and tell him the truth. I owe him a sincere apology."

"Something tells me Murdock will spring back quickly. Perhaps Lady Helen can keep him company."

Julianna slapped Rhys's shoulder, but she couldn't help her giggle. "That's awful, and you know it."

Rhys shrugged. "On the contrary. It sounds as if the man

is looking for an obedient wife. He surely hadn't found one in you."

Julianna shook her head. "You're right, actually. I'll be certain to point that out to him during my apology." She sighed. "I do regret that he'll be hurt in this. You and I never should have let each other go."

"I agree, Love," Rhys replied. "Let's never make that foolish mistake again." He leaned over and kissed her on the lips. He held her hand silently for a few moments before saying, "May I show you something?"

"Of course." She pulled the sheet up under her arms and settled back against the pillows, her hair streaming over both shoulders.

Rhys rolled over and pulled open the bedside drawer. When he rolled back, he was holding something small and white in his hand.

He opened his palm to show her.

Julianna glanced down to see a handkerchief. "Mine?" she asked.

"Yes," he nodded, "the one you gave me the night before I left for France. I kept it with me all those weeks. Even after I was angry with you, I couldn't make myself discard it. It smells like you...lilacs."

Julianna leaned over and kissed him. "Do you know, I still have the handkerchief I took from your study, also?"

"No." He smiled at her. "Where is it?"

"Hidden in a reticule in my wardrobe." She laughed and kissed him again. "It smells like you, too."

They both laughed and then Julianna said, "Oh, wait till you hear that Mary knew who you were the whole time. Can you believe it?"

Rhys threw back his head and laughed. "Ha. Are you serious? If so, she's a fine actress, your sister."

"That's what I told her. I never had an inkling that she knew." Julianna shook her head.

Rhys placed the handkerchief back on the side table. "She didn't wonder why I was pretending to be a groomsman?"

Julianna shrugged. "That's Mary for you."

Rhys gathered Julianna in his arms again. "I wasn't jesting about the buttercups. I fully intend to purchase a hothouse full of them for her. And I may offer Clayton an ungodly sum of money to buy Whisper for her, too."

Tears sprang to Julianna's eyes. "You'd do that for her?"

He rubbed her shoulder. "Of course I would."

A sly smile covered Julianna's face. "Well, in that case, you may want to leave Whisper where she is, and we'll simply take Mary back to Clayton Manor for more lessons."

At Rhys's confused look, Julianna continued, "Seems Lady Mary fancies a certain groomsman named Henry."

Rhys's eyebrows shot up. "Are you jesting?"

"Not at all. She confessed to me after we returned. Apparently, he gave her another riding lesson after I came back to London."

Rhys shook his head. "Well, I can hardly blame Henry. But I can't see your father being pleased with the match."

"You might be surprised. I've come to learn recently that while Mary may seem quiet, she has a spine a blacksmith couldn't bend with fire."

"I don't doubt it. She is your sister, after all."

NOT AN HOUR LATER, a loud banging on the front door woke Rhys out of a deep, contented sleep. *Blast.* No doubt Julianna's father was at the door. Well, Rhys might as well be called on the carpet. It was bound to happen sooner than later.

Careful not to wake Julianna, Rhys quickly slipped out of

the bed and pulled on a dressing gown. Then, he hobbled his way down the stairs where a sleepy-sounding Lawson—also garbed in a dressing gown—had already opened the front door.

"I don't care what time it is, let me in," came Bell's urgent voice from outside.

"My master is asleep, my lord," Lawson replied. "I will tell him you were here."

"It's all right, Lawson," Rhys called, somewhat relieved that it was merely the Marquess of Bellingham and not the Duke of Montlake, here to challenge him to pistols at dawn. "Let him in."

Lawson dutifully stepped back and opened the door wider, bowing to the marquess.

Bell marched inside, with a diminutive, pretty, young redheaded woman at his side. Rhys narrowed his eyes on her. She looked vaguely familiar. Was she one of the lady's maids from Clayton's house party? He'd seen her a time or two during meals in the manor house.

Rhys braced a hand on the bottom of the balustrade and blinked. "Care to tell me why you're here at this hour, Bell?"

Bell's face looked grim. "We've found the Bidassoa traitor. We need to leave for France immediately, and we need your help."

Thank you for reading *Duke Looks Like a Groomsman*. Please page forward to see related books, my biography, and how to contact me!
Valerie

ALSO BY VALERIE BOWMAN

The Footmen's Club

The Footman and I (Book 1)

Duke Looks Like a Groomsman (Book 2)

The Valet Who Loved Me (Book 3)

Save a Horse, Ride a Viscount (Book 4)

Playful Brides

The Unexpected Duchess (Book 1)

The Accidental Countess (Book 2)

The Unlikely Lady (Book 3)

The Irresistible Rogue (Book 4)

The Unforgettable Hero (Book 4.5)

The Untamed Earl (Book 5)

The Legendary Lord (Book 6)

Never Trust a Pirate (Book 7)

The Right Kind of Rogue (Book 8)

A Duke Like No Other (Book 9)

Kiss Me At Christmas (Book 10)

Mr. Hunt, I Presume (Book 10.5)

No Other Duke But You (Book 11)

Secret Brides

Secrets of a Wedding Night (Book 1)

A Secret Proposal (Book 1.5)

Secrets of a Runaway Bride (Book 2)

A Secret Affair (Book 2.5)

Secrets of a Scandalous Marriage (Book 3)

It Happened Under the Mistletoe (Book 3.5)

Thank you for reading *Duke Looks Like a Groomsman*. I hope you enjoyed Rhys's and Julianna's story.
There are few types of stories I like better than a tale of reunited lovers and these two were so much fun to write about.

I'd love to keep in touch.

- Visit my website for information about upcoming books, excerpts, and to sign up for my email newsletter: www.ValerieBowmanBooks.com or at www.ValerieBowmanBooks.com/subscribe.
- Join me on Facebook: http://Facebook.com/ValerieBowmanAuthor.
- Reviews help other readers find books. I appreciate all reviews whether positive or negative. Thank you so much for considering it!

Want to read the other Footmen's Club books?

- The Footman and I
- The Valet Who Loved Me
- Save a Horse, Ride a Viscount

ABOUT THE AUTHOR

Valerie Bowman grew up in Illinois with six sisters (she's number seven) and a huge supply of historical romance novels.

After a cold and snowy stint earning a degree in English with a minor in history at Smith College, she moved to Florida the first chance she got.

Valerie now lives in Jacksonville with her family including her two rascally dogs. When she's not writing, she keeps busy reading, traveling, or vacillating between watching crazy reality TV and PBS.

Valerie loves to hear from readers. Find her on the web at www.ValerieBowmanBooks.com.

facebook.com/ValerieBowmanAuthor

twitter.com/ValerieGBowman

instagram.com/valeriegbowman

goodreads.com/Valerie_Bowman

pinterest.com/ValerieGBowman

bookbub.com/authors/valerie-bowman

amazon.com/author/valeriebowman

CPSIA information can be obtained
at www.ICGtesting.com
Printed in the USA
LVHW091646130521
687356LV00008B/887